Paige was unbuttoning her shirt . . . Moni's heart rate raced ahead in nervous anticipation. The flesh of Paige's breasts, held tightly in a skimpy black bra, flashed boldly into the open as she whipped the shirt from her shoulders. Shouts erupted from every direction. And Paige responded, wetting her thumb and index finger with her tongue and gently squeezing a black-clad nipple between them.

DAWN OF THE DANCE

BY

MARIANNE K.
MARTIN

THE NAIAD PRESS, INC.
1999

Printed in the United States of America on acid-free paper
First Edition

Editor: Lila Empson
Cover designer: Bonnie Liss (Phoenix Graphics)
Typesetter: Sandi Stancil

Library of Congress Cataloging-in-Publication Data

Martin, Marianne K., 1945 –
    Dawn of the dance / by Marianne K. Martin.
        p.   cm.
    ISBN 1-56280-229-1   (alk. paper)
    I. Title.
PS3563.A7258D39   1999
813'.54—dc21

98-44749
CIP

For Jo

Acknowledgments

A heartfelt thank you, long overdue, to Joyce B., Nancy, Jan, Ginny, Jo Ellen, Mary Lou B., Kay, Carol, Dede, and Barb for being a special part of my life. You have made it rich beyond your knowledge.

And special thank yous to my friend Shannon, whose expertise I depend upon; to Theresa and Donna for the dance; and to my partner and best friend, Jo, for her love and commitment and for never tiring of my stories.

About the Author

Marianne Martin currently resides in Michigan as a writer and professional photographer. After many years of teaching in the public school system, she first turned her hobbies into a career as a photojournalist with the *Michigan Women's Times*. An athlete since childhood, she has been a successful basketball and softball coach at the high school and amateur levels, and field hockey coach at the collegiate level. All her not-so-leisure time in recent years has been spent working with her father to design and build her own home. The experience, wrapped around bruises, splinters, and a powerful sense of accomplishment, has taught her more about herself than she ever would have guessed.

She is the author of *Legacy of Love* and *Love in the Balance*, both published by Naiad Press. Her short stories are included in Naiad's 1997 and 1998 anthologies, *Lady Be Good* and *The Touch of Your Hand*.

Young life, tender and thinly sheathed, shuddering against the sting of winter's breath, struggled alone to bear the length of its seasons. Survival rested ostensibly on the warm coaxing of a southern whisper. Fate's secret unforetold.

ONE

The painful truth was that Monica Matteson was too old for her years and too young for her dreams. But knowing it earlier would not have changed her life, she admitted, walking the stretch of sidewalk past her old high school as if a late bell still mattered.

From behind her, male voices were carried on strides longer than her own and jarred mocking words from her memory once again.

* * * * *

"Let's walk Moni home."

"Yeah, she's carrying all those heavy books. You need some help?" One of the boys grabbed the books from her arms and began throwing them like Frisbees, one by one, into the street. Her protests only made them laugh harder and throw farther. She started for the street, trying to beat the changing light, but the boys held her tightly by the arms while the tires of passing cars bumped over her books like unavoidable potholes.

Minutes later, between breaks in traffic and with tears dripping from her cheeks, Moni hurriedly gathered the books and damaged papers. The taunts of the boys changed to howls of laughter as she fished her library book from the muddy pool of water along the opposite curb. Tearfully she warned God again that she could not stand another day.

Moni stepped from the sidewalk momentarily. The voices continued without a break, and the boys in the red-and-black varsity jackets moved swiftly past. They had no intention of taking her books or playing tug-of-war with her jacket until the sleeves gave at the seams. She preferred seeing their backs, nonetheless.

While she paid closer than usual attention to a place she'd rather forget, spring's warm breath awakened yellow blooms of forsythia and a surprising sense of nostalgia. *Funny*, she thought, *how what you feel affects what you see. Really see, that is. How you can look at something for years and only see what you feel.*

Every day for years, as she approached those

dreaded doors, she searched the surrealistic fingers of ivy that caressed the school's old brick edifice until she found the form of the running woman with tight-leafed hair streaming behind her. She realized now that she *had been* the running woman. Maybe she still was.

Without realizing it, Moni began walking the familiar path, as if with sketchbook and pass, toward the courtyard next door. She wound around exquisitely manicured bushes and beds of crocus whites and forget-me-not blues, past concrete benches tucked into privet niches, to a small pond at the courtyard's center, and settled onto her favorite bench.

She had always felt nurtured here. Her soul empowered by the promises of spring; her heart allowed the pondering of any dream her mind could imagine. Many times she had sat here, her pencil gliding effortlessly over the page. Those had been the cherished times, uninterrupted, unencumbered by social pressure. Times free of pain. Here it didn't matter that her peers would never accept her, that socially there had been nothing comfortable about school since the fifth grade.

She had been on good days ignored, on others the brunt of tasteless jokes or cruel innuendoes. They all hurt — the name-calling, the notes in her locker, the slam books. And nothing she tried had stopped them.

She had stopped telling her parents in the seventh grade. She couldn't stand what she saw in their eyes. *Why would anyone want to hurt their little girl that way?* But, getting through one more day was more important than knowing why. So she had varied her path home every day and looked for places to tuck the fear and the anger. She had hidden them under pastel

3

chalk and behind an irrepressible drive to achieve. Her artwork earned her recognition at national conventions and a scholarship to the university. Swimming earned her a Water Saving Instructor's certificate to teach, and the respect of Jean Kesh, who was always more than a teacher and never less than a friend. Without Jean, without Mr. Sands and his nurturing of her shy expression, she never would have made it. Yet despite them the time hadn't passed quickly enough.

Resting folded arms across her knees, Moni looked down into the water. *Who is this young woman looking back at me? With the slow-to-smile eyes and the Eddie Bauer shirt? A scholarship student. A frozen face at a masquerade dance.* She was who she had to be now. But she would never forget the little girl in someone else's clothes, or what she had been through. And she doubted her ability to forgive.

TWO

Moni brought the old Escort to rest in front of the house on High Street. Out of habit she combed her fingers through wind-whipped hair. But there was no need to get out of the car. The sign in the front yard announced the house was for sale. This time, though, she was sure the sign had been placed there with the full knowledge and consent of the owner, and not by a softball team with an insatiable appetite for practical jokes. With a smile she wondered how Lou Ann, or any coach, had endured the pranks of such a group and not entertained at least one homicidal plan.

Before Lou Ann knew it, the team had taken over her house, and from Sunday to Sunday made it their home away from home. They brought her food raided from fruit stands, used her kitchen at all hours of the day, and cluttered her bathroom with unidentifiable toiletries. Yet, they made her laugh — at pranks and jokes and collapsing human pyramids. And as athletes, they worked hard to make her proud. They were a displaced brood of chicks and she the mother hen who met their problems, however trivial or potentially disastrous, with understanding and wisdom.

There were toys in the driveway now, and strangers living in what used to be her world, yet she could see it as clearly now as the day she had found it. She had entered that door, like Alice in Wonderland, into a world that had only existed in her dreams. Each day she had claimed a little more of it until finally the night came when it began claiming her.

That night, from her favorite spot in the overstuffed chair in the corner, she watched the others dancing in the dining room. She loved to watch them — laughing, and singing. Sometimes she envied them. They seemed not to have the same straps of fear that bound Moni to the familiar. They wandered about the house freely, ate on their feet, danced spontaneously. Moni never wandered. She left her seat only with purpose, to get a Coke or a hamburger or to go to the bathroom. Otherwise, she watched and listened.

As she did at every party, Moni searched through the moving mass for the head of dark, cropped hair with its shock of blonde streaks. This year's new center fielder with a body everyone wanted and no one deserved, and a knee-high throw from center to home. She smiled at the sight of her. Paige Flemming, arms above her head, body moving as though she had written the music herself. She was sensuality in full motion, Moni's favorite fantasy now.

At first Moni couldn't watch herself practice, even in the privacy of her own bedroom. With eyes closed she stood before her mirror, listening to the music, visualizing Paige's movements, afraid to destroy the image by opening her eyes. Night after night she practiced, letting the music tell her when to move, filling her with excitement, until it finally felt good enough to look. Maybe someday what she saw really would be good enough. And then she would dance.

"Clear the floor, ladies. Come on, come on," Carol commanded, waving a tape in her hand. "I think Paige is drunk enough to dance." She clicked the tape in place and at the first suggestive notes the women began gathering on the floor in the big open space between the two rooms.

Moni sent a questioning look at the right fielder as she knelt beside her. "The hottest striptease you'll ever see," she replied. "They stand on bar tables to see a butch with a body like that."

Suddenly Paige came backing through the door with Carol's hands firmly gripping her shoulders. "Dammit, Carol! I'm not dancing!" She struggled under the sturdy catcher's strong grasp, but her protest went unrecognized. The women shouted and whistled, and Carol gave her a final push into the middle of the room. "Lou Ann," Paige pleaded.

Moni winced. She wanted to stand up and tell her

she didn't have to dance, to tell them to leave her alone. The words were somewhere in her head, shouting out at her, but they found no voice.

Paige's hands slipped from her hips with resolve. For the first few seconds she listened to the cheering women and the beginning of the rewound tape. Then her head dropped back submissively, and slowly the rhythm of the music brought life to her body. Hips, clad in tight jeans, began gliding sensuously from side to side. One shoulder, then the other, shrugged upward to pull an open palm over her hip and up her side, pressing spread-fingered against the side of her breast. Then she turned, eyes focused somewhere over the heads of the crowd, while leggy strides brought her closer. Her hands continued over the flowing curves of a body that had become a vision in sensuous sound. The music never left her hips, her shoulders, and her head; the notes pulsed their lifeblood through them.

Moni stared, mesmerized, barely aware of the tingling warmth seeping from the pores of her body. Never had she seen anyone move with such fluidity. Every inch of Paige's body rippled and flowed, not in response to the music but rather in interpretation of it. In the framework of sensuality, she was showing the world how the music felt. The only thing capable of snatching Moni from her trance was the realization that Paige was unbuttoning her shirt.

Fingers teased and opened button after button while Moni's heart rate raced ahead in nervous anticipation. The flesh of Paige's breasts, held tightly in a skimpy black bra, flashed boldly into the open as she whipped the shirt from her shoulders. Shouts erupted from every direction. And Paige responded, wetting her thumb and index finger with her tongue and gently squeezing a black-clad nipple between them.

Moni blushed an even brighter shade of red. Despite how it made her feel physically, she wanted to look away. She didn't want to see her like this, mocking the beauty of her own body as if it meant no more to her than a stained old T-shirt. But she couldn't pull her eyes away. Paige continued her unmerciful tease, sliding her loose shirt across her buttocks as they moved from side to side. She swung it over her head and drew it so slowly up between her legs. Once. Twice. Then she stretched it above her shoulders and lowered her hips, circling them just beyond reach. Women's hands appeared from everywhere, reaching for her legs and higher. Coyly she avoided them, hips in constant motion, her own hands touching what theirs could not. She slid them down her thighs and up the inside, drawing a finger slowly over her zipper. Then she lowered herself even farther. Hands, spread wide, traveled down her thighs again. And again up the inside, this time stopping to cover the seam below her zipper while her hips ground in small circles against it. The women lost all reserve.

"Aw, baby, let me help," someone shouted.

With an exasperating rebuff, Paige rose and stepped the distance of a turn from the grasping hands. Yet she tormented them still, spreading her arms wide and shimmying her chest and shoulders to their accompanying moans.

As hard as it was for her to tear her eyes from the movement of Paige's body, Moni forced herself to look up into her face. Mannequin eyes stared out over the room, their lids opening and closing mechanically. Lips the color of natural blush formed a tight line. Paige's

9

plea to Lou Ann sounded through her thoughts. Moni looked once more into the expressionless eyes — and she knew. The exhibitionism and the alcohol were only camouflage. *Good* camouflage, hiding fears with a gift so persuasive that it gave the exact opposite impression. But Moni knew. Paige, too, was afraid.

Suddenly someone squealed beside her. Paige was moving toward them, and in the space of a short breath her hips were eye level, motions of silk on silk pressing toward Moni's face. She heard herself swallow as fingers came to the closure of Paige's jeans. And instantly the snap lay open; the zipper tab stood exposed.

"Do it, Moni," someone insisted, as Moni felt Paige's shirt drop around her neck and pull her forward. Her heart beat nervously as she looked up into eyes that did not expect to be met. The dark pupils of Paige's eyes widened until the blue-gray was only a thin ring. Then with one blink the glassy shade that covered them was lifted, along with her shirt.

Another young woman nudged her aside, and slipped close between Paige's legs. But as she leaned forward to grasp the zipper, Paige placed her hand against the woman's forehead and pushed her backward. With a practiced arrogance she moved on to the dark-haired second-base woman, who slid between her legs, grasped the zipper tab with her teeth, and pulled it down. As chants of her name goaded her courage, the woman clasped Paige's buttocks and buried her face in the exposed flesh. And in the next instant, she too was pushed backward into supporting arms.

"Moni, if your pants are dry, they're the only ones in the room that are," someone behind her quipped.

The comment left her puzzled. She knew only that every piece of clothing she had on was soaked. Whatever sexual connotation was intended, and she was sure it was, would be figured out later, in her own good time. For now, she had no intention of letting anyone know what she did or did not understand. As she always had, she would watch and listen, and sooner or later it would all make sense. Just how soon would surprise her.

Paige emerged from the back porch and dropped a beer bottle into the empties box. Lou Ann motioned in her direction. "There's who you should get to pose for you, Moni."

Contemptuously Paige responded, "Yeah, that's a new one. 'Take your clothes off, I want to draw you.'"

Moni answered softly, "I'd want to do your face." If she hadn't known her secret, the look she received from Paige as she abruptly left the kitchen would have struck painfully. But nothing these women could do would ever hurt her; she was sure of that. They were too much like her. Especially Paige Flemming, who had in her soul something that spoke to Moni without words. Something that made her sensitive to the injustices of life, no matter how small. The same thing that spawned the many cloaks of camouflage, and hid her pain from the world.

Only one couple remained, moving slowly to the music as Moni crossed the dining room. Unexpectedly, someone grabbed her arm and turned her. Without a word, without time to say no, Moni's hands were placed around Paige's neck, and Paige's hands were sliding down her arms. And down her sides, touching ever so slightly there against her breasts, and slowly down to her waist. Forehead pressed to Moni's, Paige made no eye contact, only moved her hands again to direct Moni's hips against her own.

A sensation like no other she'd ever felt shot through Moni's body. It felt like a jolt of electrical current from a frayed wire, only stronger, its effects more lasting. Where their bodies touched she could feel nothing but heat searing through her jeans. Slowly, guided by the hands that held them, her hips moved tighter into the heat that fused them. While Moni's heart pounded wildly against her chest, the rhythm of the music coursed through Paige's body and into her own. Never had she imagined that dancing slow would feel like this. Nor had she known, as much as she had yearned for the feel of another woman's body against her, that it would feel this good. The shakiness of her body, the weakness of her legs, she figured had more to do with excitement than fear. She was not afraid, maybe worried about her own short-comings, but definitely not afraid of this woman.

Paige's arms circled Moni's hips and back and pulled her against the full length of her body. She pressed her face to the side of Moni's head. Her breath, which had smelled of alcohol, now touched warmly over her ear. Less concerned now about her own, Moni finally took a normal breath. But as they moved, she found it difficult to take anything but short, shallow whiffs of air. Her body, it seemed, had a disposition all its own. It was doing things she had never felt before, things she had no control over: the heat, the shakiness, and the perspiration running down her sides. And the strange feeling low in her abdomen that at first felt like the beginning ache of her menstrual cycle. But it grew in intensity, like the heat radiating through her body from the pressure of Paige's thigh. And Moni knew, without question, that she was being sexually aroused for the first time.

All the while Paige held her and moved her, all the while her body unfolded its excitement, the questions lingered in Moni's mind. *Was this what everyone felt when they danced this close? Did the heat from Paige's body mean she was feeling the same things? And what was supposed to happen from here?* She had no answers, and certainly no intention of asking. She wished only that her mind could ignore them and leave her awakened body to enjoy its first sparks of desire in innocent anonymity.

If it meant that none of this would end, the music, the embrace, the wonderful way her body felt, she would keep her eyes closed tightly forever. But the last notes of the song began to fade sadly into the empty room. Paige slid her hands up Moni's back and held her tightly as their bodies stilled. For long seconds she said nothing, her cheek pressed against Moni's ear. Then the question was whispered softly. "Do you really want to draw me?"

"Yes." *And whatever else it takes to see you again.*

Her eyes finally met Moni's as she released their embrace. "One-twenty-seven Blackstone."

THREE

One-twenty-seven Blackstone looked no different from the outside. Its sun-washed paint was chalk green. Its screened porch still yawned its welcome only a few feet from the walk. The scent of wild catnip no doubt still whirled through the noisy blades of the window fan to make Paige's old room still smell of mint. A room. Just that and no more. Four rented walls that housed a double bed, a near-antique bureau, and a chair with flowered upholstery that testified to its years of service. No clutter. Only a newspaper, a pair of glasses, and a handful of change. An outdated motel room, minus the suitcase. Now another renter called it home. Nothing but memories remained to remind her of a world she thought would always be there.

The day she first came here to draw now seemed so long ago. She had come to record the truth beyond the drunken laughter, the dancing, and the moody stares. And she had done that, in the tilt of Paige's head, the angle of her shoulders, in the eyes that knew things but refused to tell. In line and shadow she analyzed the face of the woman who danced in her daydreams, and found what she wanted. When she finished, Moni came back for another pose; then she came back just to be there. To work crossword puzzles or the tarot cards while Ella Fitzgerald sang them the blues. To fit herself neatly into Paige's life.

"That you, Moni?" The voice barely reached the car from the porch, where an old woman half filled the width of a porch glider.

As Moni approached the steps, the woman continued with scarcely more than the effort it took to breathe. "Come on up here. Ain't lettin' you go on without talking to old Maiva."

"How have you been?"

Maiva rubbed a paper napkin, wet with the sweat of her glass, under her chin and around to the back of her neck. "Child, you oughta know better than to ask that of an old lady . . . You're wonderin' about Paige is my bet."

"*And* you. Didn't the cards tell you that?"

"Ahh, neither one'll do ya no good." She brushed a newspaper, folded to the crossword puzzle, off her lap onto the seat next to her. "Ain't been a renter since, kin finish a crossword puzzle like that girl. Never even finished high school . . . Here now, you go git your- self some lemonade."

"I'm on my way back to school. I can't stay long."

"Just as well," she said, and took a long drink from her glass. "Don't wanna git used to havin' ya around."

No. They'd both done that once. And loneliness was all it had gotten them. A lesson that taught her that what was accepted in your head wasn't necessarily accepted in your heart. It wasn't by her choice that she had stopped coming by. She wasn't even sure it had been Paige's. All she knew were the facts as Lou Ann had explained them.

"I'm not sure how to say this, Moni." The night was menthol cool. The scents and sounds of summer drifted from open doors and rolled-down car windows. But Lou Ann's voice carried a tone that shut it all out. "Paige likes you. She likes you a lot." She cleared her throat and continued her thoughtful pace. "But you're too young, Moni. Do you know what I'm saying?"

She knew immediately. One of the rules was being enforced, part of the unwritten, unofficial code that included no drugs, and no one underage smoking or drinking.

"You'll still be friends and play ball together. But that's all it can be. I hope you understand."

* * * * *

16

Part of her had understood, even then. But under-standing didn't take away the yearning that only the next time in Paige's arms could satisfy, and it didn't ease the emptiness. *How do you explain that to an old woman?*

"I missed coming over here, Maiva. It's not that I didn't want to . . . between working at the recreation department during the day and the Y at night, and not wanting to give up softball. Even my family didn't see me much."

"I figured Paige got in a twit and hurt your feelings." Her eyes followed a faded blue Mazda, threading its way between parked cars. A gravelly sound started in Maiva's throat. Moni could never tell, for a second or two, if was to be a cough or a laugh. This time it was a laugh. "Sometimes I start re-memberin', and it makes me laugh. Do you remember what you girls did to poor ole Jenkins that day at the lake? Poor ole lush."

Moni's grin emerged into a full smile. "He'd been drinking steadily all day. It always embarrassed Bonnie so much."

"Yer damn lucky he didn't keel over right there from a heart attack."

"You should've seen his face, Maiva. It was worth the risk. All six-foot-five of him was stretched out over that lounge chair, snorin' so loud you could've heard him on the other side of the lake. It was Bonnie's idea. Eight of us surrounded his chair, picked it up on the same count, and carried him, without a sound, without even a jostle, out into the lake until the water reached the chair. Then we let go of it and ran like hell. When we got up on the beach and looked back, he was still sinking, eyes closed, mouth wide open. Then he came to, sputtering and swearing, those long skinny arms and legs thrashin' around. We were all doubled up in laughter. As soon as he got his bearings, the old scarecrow chased us up and down that beach till we thought he'd die."

Maiva laughed herself right into a cough. "I thought he musta caught some of you. Paige's clothes were still wet when she got home."

"No, we did that to ourselves. Bonnie thought the least we could do for her poor old dad was buy him a pack of cigarettes, since his last pack was floating in the lake. Everyone decided to walk to the party store on the other side of the lake. But Bonnie headed right toward the water. 'Come on,' she said, 'this lake's shallow enough to walk all the way across.' So in we went, clothes and all."

"Paige don't even swim."

"She was hissin' and spittin' like a cat in a bathtub all the way across. Holding her cigarettes and lighter out of the water and swearing that she was gonna live to kill someone."

Maiva rumbled into another laugh.

"But, best of all was the look on the faces of the people on the public beach as the whole team emerged from the lake like the Loch Ness monster."

She eased out of her laugh with a little cough. "Never told me that part. That girl could come home with stories to give this heart of mine a real good laugh. Didn't much care if they were true or not."

"Chances are they were true." Maiva reached for her glass, while Moni fidgeted, opening and closing the clasp on her key ring. "Do you know where she went?"

"Canada, I think. Just picked up and left. The day after that big party. Remember that? Ain't seen her since . . . Just as well, I guess. Don't need the worry."

Moni nodded as she rose. "I miss her, too," she said, leaning down to place a kiss on the old woman's damp cheek. "I'll be back to visit next time I'm in town."

FOUR

The Escort labored through its gears and merged behind a semi onto I-94. Moni pushed the preset button to the oldies station, although she'd promised herself she wouldn't listen to it anymore. It would be part of her self-induced therapy. *Revisit that part of your life and claim control over it.* Exactly what she was doing. Remembering it all — the good, the bad, and the painful — head-on. All that was left now was the end of the fantasy.

The long weekend party, the end of the summer.

20

By then she had recognized that what was between her and Paige was a kind of virtual reality game. But it was one she was ill prepared to play. Cat became mouse and knew how to run. Mouse became cat with no idea how to chase.

As had become usual, Paige kept a comfortable distance all day that Saturday and into the evening. She wrapped dancing around jokes and laughs and drinks, but not around Moni. So whenever the mouse stopped in a deceptive tease, the counterfeit cat feigned indifference. It was less painful that way. Clearly, chasing something that can't be caught only gives credence to a demoralizing chase and strips dignity to the bone. Being chased is much more dignified. How fast someone runs is up to her. Either way, it's an exhausting game. Moni started toward the kitchen for a break.

Lou Ann stopped her at the doorway. "Moni, it looks like everyone is going to the bar shortly. I'm not sure what to do with you. Any other night we could get you in on a promise not to drink, but Granny follows the law to the letter in her place, and it's too busy a night."

"That's all right. I understand."

"Do you want me to stay here with you?"

"No, really, I'll be fine. Just show me where the videos are, and I'll watch movies."

Forty-five minutes later, Moni wandered alone through the rambling ranch house. The muted desert hues of its southwestern design had gone practically unnoticed behind the constant bustle of bodies. It seemed to breathe an expansive sigh as the last of the women left its doors.

She imagined this was her house as she fluffed the pillows back in place on the couch and straightened the magazines on the table. *Yes, I'll subscribe to* Girlfriends, *too. And then slip them under the couch when my folks visit.*

She scanned the bookshelves and read each of the video jackets. She placed *Therese and Isabelle* next to the VCR before heading for the kitchen. She took a Coke-shaped glass from the cupboard and a Coke from the refrigerator. *Granny would not have had to worry about her. Jenny was probably on her second Kahlúa mudslide right now.* But there are worse things than not going to the bar, she reminded herself, filling her glass with ice cubes. *It was nothing personal, just poor planning.*

Suddenly a hand appeared from behind her and covered her glass. She jumped with fright. "I'd have you fill my glass, too, but you're dangerous with ice cubes."

"God, Paige! You scared the piss out of me!" she declared into the half-grinning face. "What are you doing here anyway?"

"Trying to sleep. The Motrin didn't help my cramps."

"I had no ID."

The grin disappeared. Paige took her eyes abruptly from Moni's. "Would you fix me a drink?"

Paige sipped the vodka and tonic, mixed per her directions, and sorted through a stack of tapes. The vision fit perfectly into Moni's fantasy of private weekends away from school spent with Paige in an apartment somewhere near . . . anywhere. She was looking for reasons to believe someday that it could be more than a fantasy.

The tape, with its handwritten index of classic love songs, was the one they played at the end of every party. Paige clicked it into place and took Moni's hands as she had so many times during the first part of the summer. This time though, they were alone. And the eyes that looked at her now no longer held their mannequin stare. Their directness sent a shock wave through Moni more arousing than her touch.

With both hands in hers, Paige wrapped them around the small of Moni's back and pressed the length of their bodies tightly together. Moni closed her eyes and allowed herself to feel what she had missed so much. They moved very little, in what was more an embrace set to music than a dance. Not a word passed between them. Paige, she knew, was speaking with her body. Moni was trying to answer with hers.

When the song ended Paige released her embrace but continued holding Moni's hands silently between them. This wouldn't be their only dance tonight. Moni looked up from their hands and met Paige's eyes at the first notes of "Unchained Melody." She had never heard a more sensuous love song, nor received a more intimate look than was in Paige's eyes. This time Paige did not look away. She raised Moni's hands and placed them around her neck, just as she had that very first night. The same magical current emanating from her eyes now passed through her hands as they drew slowly down Moni's arms and sides and came to rest on her hips. Paige held her this way for what seemed an eternity, cheek to Moni's forehead, hips held inches away, guided to the music with her hands.

The heat between them grew with the honesty of the words, words speaking of the hunger in Moni's own heart and the hunger she hoped was in Paige's.

With the swell of the music, the words rose like a tidal wave inside her, struggling against Moni's inability to say them aloud. The need to whisper them along with the song was almost too much to bear. Yet the fear that Paige would reject them held fortress-like. If they were to be spoken, it would have to be by Paige, in whatever way she could.

Words of passion filled the air, crescendoing in a powerful symphony, and at least one decision was made. Paige pulled Moni's hips against her own, nestled her into the firm full breasts. Moni responded by embracing the broad shoulders, her fingers caressing the back of Paige's neck and her hair. Words she'd waited a lifetime to hear were whispered into her ear. "I missed you."

Such sweet words. Stabbing a pain through the center of her chest. Tears came to her eyes as she hugged Paige tightly and pressed her cheek to her ear. Heat radiated from Paige's body, while the beating of her heart competed with the pounding in Moni's chest. The last dramatic strains of music thinned poignantly in the air. Their bodies slowed until they were just holding each other.

It became apparent in that moment that the need to be in Paige's arms had become much more than that. It had blended, almost unnoticed, into the ache that began with her touch. The arousal was familiar, but tonight the power of it surprised her. Stronger than the beating of her heart, it pushed down walls and pressed its rhythm into Paige's hips. Moni broke the trance of silent emotion, moving sensuously to another love song, and initiated the next stage of seduction.

Paige's hands slid the length of Moni's sides, encircled her buttocks, and joined the slow movement of her hips. "You're making me crazy," Paige whispered, pressing her lips into Moni's neck.

Hands, spread over Moni's buttocks, now pressed her to Paige's pelvis with each beat of the music. The pressure of her thigh stoked a fire so intense it made Moni's legs weak beneath her. She clung to Paige with a moan of pleasure she hadn't meant to utter. Its answer came only beats later when Paige stilled their bodies and buried a moan in Moni's neck. Her body was so warm and wet and out of control that Moni dared return the kiss to the salty skin of Paige's neck. She prayed for Paige to want her, to kiss her with a need even half as much.

But short seconds later, Paige released their embrace without a word and stepped away. *No, Paige,* she pleaded si*lently, please don't stop. I'll never be able to say how much I need you.*

For a long moment, Paige stared into her eyes, long enough for Moni to know that once again she would be left to ache alone. She took a deep breath and began fighting the tears she would cry later.

Then Paige reached down and took her hand. She led her down the hallway and leaned unsteadily against her as they entered the darkened room. Moni turned in to Paige's arms and steadied their embrace. "Are you okay?" she asked quietly.

"Maybe you shouldn't have fixed me that last drink."

The ache low in Moni's abdomen competed now with an excitement that shook her whole body. Hands, instinctively confident, were caressing her back, spreading their warmth. Before she could decide whether to initiate their first kiss, Paige's hands had traveled the length of their reach and lifted Moni onto the bed. The dizziness she felt as she lay back rivaled the effects of too many wine coolers, yet this intoxication took only the smell of alcohol on Paige's breath and the scent of the cologne that had haunted her all summer.

Leaning over her in the darkness, Paige kissed her lips for the first time. The warm soft lips that Moni had wanted for so long now pressed over her mouth, touching her lips with tenderness, opening them, and teaching them. The thrill of it reached every nerve in her body; the current it sparked countered the disbelief that this was really happening. Paige's tongue, velvety and wet, explored with a gentle probing, hurling her mind weightlessly into space. Dizzy in the darkness, Moni grasped Paige's arms and pulled her body against her, lifting her knee and accepting Paige's thigh snugly between her legs. The music from the other room found its rhythm in Paige's body, thumping its beat into Moni, illuminating her body with sensation. Paige kissed her with increasing desire, deeply, almost fiercely, while her hands appeared beneath Moni's T-shirt with lessons of their own. The first hands to uncover the virgin flesh, the first to give their pleasure.

It was all happening so quickly now. Sensations rushed from everywhere, from every place Paige touched — with her hands, her lips, her tongue — telling Moni how much she was wanted, making her believe. It was the strangest feeling she'd ever had — not knowing what was coming, but wanting it more

26

than anything in her life. Never in any fantasy could she have imagined it. Even if she had dared to ask, no one could describe what she was feeling.

Moni wanted to touch back, to feel the skin of the body that had teased her from her first sight of it, but just as she let her hand dare beneath the half-open shirt, Paige's hand found the seam of her pants. The sensation she felt, as the fingers traced the length of the seam between her legs, burst forth in a gasp, half muffled under the cover of Paige's lips. The fingers continued their titillation until wetness soaked through the material, and Moni's breaths stopped short in their rhythm. Paige's breathing quickened with excitement; the heat of her breath melted into the tender skin of Moni's neck.

The ache, even as strong as it was, had been swallowed up in a swelling exigency. Murmurs of pleasure formed deep in Moni's throat. Their sounds spilled over her control, exclaiming the effects of Paige's lips as they claimed the flesh of her neck and chest and the tenderness of her breasts.

"I know," Paige whispered back. "I know."

Before the words could register in the fog, the zipper of her pants was open, and fingers slipped easily into the silken heat. They drew back slowly, torturously, and glided through again. And again. And the fog in her mind suddenly had nothing to do with what was happening to her body. Pleasure mounted over pleasure. Her hips moved into the gliding fingers on their own, grasping for the next sensation, needing it. Excitement burst free on gasps of air, while Paige muffled a moan against her shoulder. *Is this the heaven they spoke of? The place where all feeling, all emotion, everything, centered in that one sensitive place? Am I there at last? Finally feeling everything that a lover feels?*

Yet each time Paige's hand slid through the center of her pleasure, heaven became more glorious. She eagerly took Paige's lips and tongue, now as a secondary pleasure, and wondered in her delirium how it could possibly get any better. Then it came. In the next stroke of her hand, and the next, and the next. The answer to the wonderful secret. The deflowering of a lifelong mystery, exploding into a thousand tiny fragments and slamming into the hand that ignited it. Over and over. Until it had exhausted her. When her breath finally returned, its attempts matched the rhythm of spasms that were dissolving her body into a quivering mass. The impulses to shout out her joy in full voice weren't easily restrained. Only when the impulses quieted did she realize Paige was inside, in a gentle caressing that kept the responses alive and sent them into sharp little spasms. They lasted, though much weaker now, until Paige withdrew and wrapped her in a strong embrace.

Moni snuggled against her lover, *her lover, Paige Flemming,* and the fogginess began to slowly dissipate. The joy she felt was immeasurable, just as she always knew it would be. As her breathing calmed to normal, she risked saying the words. "I love you," she whispered into the stillness.

Moni quickly snapped the radio off. "Love's not enough," she said aloud. She was on her way back to her real life, where it didn't matter anymore.

FIVE

Please don't be the grandmother today, she pleaded, waiting at the drawing table for the model to appear. Life drawing was not as enjoyable as Moni had hoped. Models coaxed off the street with the promise of enough money for a six-pack to take their clothes off are not life's most appealing visions. All last week it had been the grandmother, a woman in her sixties, sixty pounds overweight, and sporting the scars of three cesareans. *Not every model needed to be nude. Didn't Gionto know that? Wasn't it his job to realize the appeal she'd have clothed? To see what could be read in the lines of her face if we were allowed to look closely enough?* That Moni had chosen to look that close, and ignore the rest, had not pleased the egotistical Peter Gionto. During evaluation, with each student's work displayed on the wall, he had thrown Moni's on the floor, refusing to critique it. Life, it seemed, should only be seen through his limited vision.

Moni flipped through her sketchbook. There was the anorexic who prompted bets on how fast she'd fall asleep and whether she'd awake before falling off her stool. The drunk with more hair on his back than on his head. And the only one Moni wished back, with his smooth, muscular body held masterfully in such wonderful poses. But a six-pack hadn't brought *him* in, and he hadn't been back. Maybe today with a little luck . . .

Minutes later, however, her hopes were nixed when a skinny little man with long greasy hair walked into the room. He vanished into the changing cubicle to disrobe, and Moni seriously contemplated leaving. Why she decided to stay wasn't clear, maybe because the instructor was already aware of her. But for whatever reason, she stayed. As she opened her pad to a clean page the model walked past her, heading for the middle of the floor. Trailing behind him was a strong smell of body odor and dirty hair. She looked up to see him trying to pose himself on a blanket. Facing Moni's side of the circle, he placed a broomstick across his shoulders, and draped an arm over each end of the stick. That was bad enough. Then he lifted one leg and draped *it* over the end, exposing a full view of his genitals. *Shit! That does it.* She stood up and grabbed her things. *Gross little sleazeball must be high on something.*

She looked toward the door to see Mr. Gionto standing next to it, and continued walking until she reached the far side of the circle. Someone laughed as Moni placed her pad on a table with a view of the model's back, but another female student followed and sat next to her. Then only seconds later, still another woman moved. The point was made.

Despite the fact that he could hold no pose longer than five seconds, the model tried over and over to pose himself on the broomstick. As frustrating as it was, Moni made an honest attempt to draw, until the model finally gave up and fell asleep on the blanket.

With quiet defiance Moni, too, gave up. She flipped the page, shook the frustration from her mind, and let her hand move freely over the paper. Lines began to appear from memory, beautiful lines, transforming flat sterile white into graceful volume. Shades of gray blended delicately with fingertips created a warm fullness that emerged from the paper as a finely muscled thigh, a firm fleshy breast. The image began revealing itself, more vivid than a memory, as familiar as last night's dream. She hadn't intended it to be Paige, hadn't intended to feel again. But before she could stop it, something crept through her, tightening her throat to the point of pain, bringing tears to her eyes. This she didn't need . . . any more than she needed to suffer through this class.

Reactions had slipped past her control. She found

herself giving in to emotion better held for the sanctity of night. Moni wiped her tears quickly, ripped the page from the pad, and crumbled it into a tight ball.

Her life was where she wanted it, filled with promise and opportunity, and women. She thought she had successfully tucked whatever it was that haunted her, tormented her, so deeply into her memory bank that this could not happen.

She did not write unanswered letters, or listen to old love songs. She'd faced what had happened. No one had to tell her to move on with her life and forget. No one knew that better than Moni. And no one needed to hear about her sadness, or her anger or fear or loneliness. Without feeling it themselves they couldn't understand it, and they surely couldn't change it. *Can I forget because someone says to? Does my heart stop aching because someone says it should by now? And do I give up on finding a committed, lifelong love because it's too painful a search? Maybe.*

Moni had done what she must. She studied hard, worked long, partied whenever possible, and went to bed too tired to care. She found companionship here and there, learned to be quite good at insignificant social talk, enjoyed but never invested in fantasy. And somewhere along the way, amidst the small talk and late hours spent with strangers, she decided never again to give away so much of her soul to another.

She would go to Dedra's party tonight. She would dance and laugh, and even let her friend play cupid for the umpteenth time. And for a while she would forget how lonely she was.

The class was finally over. Moni gathered her things.

"You really had a problem today," came a voice from behind her.

Turning, she found Mr. Gionto waiting for a response. "I wish we had real models," she replied.

"I do too, but that's life. You're going to have to learn to deal with it."

The implication made her uncomfortable. Someone so incapable of teaching her anything about drawing had no business psychoanalyzing her. *What she chose to deal with, or not deal with, in her life was her business.*

SIX

Dedra's apartment was two blocks off campus and two blocks from the apartment. Moni decided to walk. Walking was therapeutic and refreshing and should not be reserved for men merely because it was dark. *A righteous obstinacy*, she insisted, with a watchful eye on her surroundings. She was doing her part to take back the night, just as she had taken back her life.

The streetlights swayed like bright, weighted baubles on gusts of a spring night wind. Their dancing light frolicked in a playful game of tag with the shadows of the street. The same street the three of them, Moni, Dedra, and Gina, had made their stage after the cast party last week. They were Jets that night, leaping and turning, snapping their fingers and singing. Down the middle of the deserted street, reminiscing Dedra's stunning performance in *West Side Story*. Talented, unpredictable Dedra, old for her age with a spirit so free, so baffling that her friends learned to expect the unexpected. A friend Moni knew she'd never forget no matter where life took her from here.

Their introduction, unforgettable in itself, took place two years ago as counselors at a private girls' camp.

"Moni, meet our dance instructor," said the head counselor, while Dedra George's eyes unashamedly wandered the length of Moni's body before meeting her own with a smile. Warning enough, right from the start, that a budding self-confidence and a shy demeanor were in for a serious challenge.

Waterfront instructor and dance teacher were paired together in a cabin of eight ten-year-olds for nearly three months. The challenges that produced seemed never ending, and privacy became a state of mind. Dedra's lessons on successfully breaking policy and making privacy when there is none began only a week into camp. With the kids sleeping soundly, they rendezvoused in the staff cabin at two A.M. to talk. Moonlight shone its elongated path through the screened window and outlined the frame of an empty chair as Moni walked in. In the shadows, the burning ember of Dedra's cigarette momentarily illuminated her face.

"Don't we have a light in here?" Moni asked, claiming the empty chair.

"No lights. Besides, I like the moonlight," came the approaching voice.

Then without a word of warning, Dedra was straddling Moni's lap, her arms cradling Moni's head and shoulders while her mouth, commanding and insistent, left its unmistakable message on her lips.

"What's this all about?" Moni asked, pinned and surprised.

"Just letting you know where I stand. When I like what I see I go after it."

And she had continued to go after it. All summer long she'd showered Moni with invitations, from stares across the dining table to surprise massages in her bunk at night. She'd even "accidentally" lost the top of her bathing suit on a day-off swim together, and Moni had fished it out of the lake. Yet Dedra, with the femininity of a ballerina and the aggressiveness of a New York stockbroker, had never attracted Moni sexually. She wanted only Dedra's friendship. Eventually Dedra admitted defeat, something she'd rarely done.

Now Dedra and Gina were together. The perfect couple for miniseries drama — Dedra, always only a breath away from another uninhibited escapade, and Gina, her finger on a hair-trigger Italian temper. There was never a lack of excitement. *It will be fun to see them tonight.*

Gina answered her knock. "Hi. Welcome to a Tale of Two Women. Enter at your own risk."

"What now?" Moni asked, stepping into the hallway.

"Nothing unusual. Dedra and I had an argument earlier, so she's in rare form tonight." She took Moni's arm.

"Well," Moni said and looked across the room, "she still has all her clothes on. That's a good sign."

"It's early."

Dedra was in the middle of one of her tales with a captive audience around her. When she saw Moni, she reached up her hand and winked an invitation for her traditional kiss. Moni obliged her with a kiss on the cheek, and Dedra pulled her down on the couch next to her. As she listened and laughed at Dedra's latest escapade, Moni looked around the room. There was no one there she hadn't met at least once. A diversified group of women — different majors, different careers, different colleges. *It should prove to be a very interesting evening,* Moni thought.

The party livened considerably after the lights were dimmed. Dedra danced to everything with the stylization — overstated arms, exaggerated steps — typical of a professional dancer. *Always performing,* Moni mused, watching Dedra invade the space of those around them before facing her again. "Look who's here," Dedra said, directing Moni's attention to the other side of the room.

Standing beside Gina was a tall, attractive woman with a smile that could make any student forget finals week. Her name was Carrie, a senior at State. Dedra winked and smiled, and merely shrugged her shoulders as Moni raised a suspicious eyebrow. Dedra, the anything but subtle matchmaker. Should she have expected any less?

Moni glanced over once to see Carrie still talking, and again to find her and Gina headed their way. "You shouldn't tempt fate, Dedra," Moni warned.

"What, and take all the fun out of life?"

"Just remember, we're called hopeless romantics for a reason." Actually, she liked Carrie. She was bright and personable and popular. But a very important part of the game Moni played with Dedra was not letting her know.

Dedra grabbed Gina's arm and dragged her out to dance, leaving Moni alone with Carrie.

"I won't pretend to dance fast, but I'm not too bad at the slow ones. Would you dance this one with me?"

Moni slipped into a conservative dance position with their bodies barely touching. Carrie talked comfortably and moved very little. Moni asked questions and kept her own answers brief. Before they realized it, they were halfway through another song, and Carrie hadn't even noticed. Dance number three, though, she did notice. A glance in the direction of the stereo confirmed their suspicions. Dedra was choosing the music.

"Feel like a stand-in in a *Hello, Dolly!* production?" Moni asked, looking up into Carrie's eyes.

Carrie laughed a hearty laugh and gathered Moni close. Her arms met around the small of Moni's back. She nuzzled warmly into the hair above her ear and made no further attempts at conversation. Barely moving in the middle of the room, they had become the center of attention. A fact Moni was as aware of as she was the very subtle sensuality of the woman holding her. This time when the song ended, Moni pulled away.

Carrie's hand slipped down Moni's arm to her hand. "I'm glad you're here tonight."

With a smile Moni reclaimed her hand and escaped to a deserted kitchen. She fixed herself a drink and sat alone at the empty table. Where this could go tonight was apparent. With or without the right reasons, with or without much effort on her part. But it was her decision. And maybe it should be made early, before other influences complicated things.

Too late.

"She is handsome, isn't she?" Dedra whispered from behind.

"Your point is?"

"That you think too much. You take life too seriously."

"Thank you," Moni replied, making her exit.

Moni mingled, talked with the women she knew best, and stealthily avoided Carrie's eyes, until during a dance with Gina, she accidentally met them head-on. For the next half-hour Carrie attempted tactfully to work her way over to Moni. She would successfully escape one woman, and another would start talking to her. Then when it looked like she was actually on her way, someone grabbed her arm to dance. A look of helplessness and a halfhearted attempt at doing the "Macarena" made Moni smile. It hadn't had a chance to fade naturally when she was snatched from her seat and pulled into the kitchen.

"All right!" she declared as Dedra pushed her into a chair. "You're really too much tonight, Dedra. I'm quite capable of running my own life, thank you."

"Then tell me what's wrong with the picture I see." Moni leaned her head against the wall and closed her eyes. "Look at those women," Dedra continued. "There's not one of them who wouldn't jump in bed with her if they had the chance. Or haven't you noticed? But who does she want, Moni? You."

"She doesn't even know me."

"No, and you're not going to let her, are you? I know how you are." She leaned down close to Moni's face. "Never let anyone get too close. Never let them have a chance to hurt you."

"The woman with all the answers."

Dedra, of course, was undaunted. She straightened with an air of over-dramatization. "I know you aren't interested in anyone in your department. You didn't like either of the jocks, or the psychology major, or the history teacher . . ." Moni gave her a look of disgust. "Okay, I agree with you on the history teacher. But dammit, Moni, what do you want?"

Moni hesitated thoughtfully while she pushed the saltshaker like a hockey puck from hand to hand. "Maybe what isn't possible."

Dedra's tone was disgustingly parental, her warning probably all too true. "Well, you sure as hell better get over that, babe, or you're going to be one lonely woman."

Moni stared out at the room of women silently. Two long drags of her cigarette later, Dedra finally asked, "Why don't you give Carrie a chance?"

"For what? A morning-after this time that takes more of me than I can afford to lose?"

"They aren't all one-night stands, Moni."

"One night, five nights, twenty nights . . . there's always a morning after." Moni turned to leave.

From the doorway of the kitchen, Dedra watched

her make her way across the room and sit next to Carrie.

Sitting there, even in the midst of the conversation, it all seemed strangely remote. For some time Moni's thoughts wandered privately, searching for a reason to go home, wondering why she didn't. She smiled at the right times but wasn't really listening. Absently, she caught a wink from Dedra. *Damn your presumptuousness, Dedra George. Yes, you're damn right they won't get too close. I'll keep my insignificant fears to myself, thank you — along with everything else. And when feelings change — theirs, mine, yours — it won't matter. So maybe loneliness is the consequence. Maybe it's unavoidable. Maybe you're right.*

Carrie's voice broke her thoughts. "You're awfully quiet."

"I'm sorry," Moni apologized, not quite aware of how long Carrie's arm had been around her.

"Dance with me again."

Carrie took her in her arms. Her voice was soothing and confident, and without willing it Moni felt the barriers begin to slip. *Isn't not making a decision, a decision?*

Long arms pulled her close and wrapped themselves around Moni's back. She lowered her own arms around Carrie's waist, and accepted the strength and confidence of their embrace.

Slowly and silently they moved, while the sounds of the party continued around them. As she had done earlier, Carrie gently nuzzled the hair over Moni's ear. And when her movements became kisses, touching heated breath to her ear and her neck, the warmth descended to the rest of Moni's body. *How much easier it would be to just turn off my mind and let my body make the decisions.* At her first opportunity, Carrie found Moni's lips. Lips soft and warm, but hesitant in their response. "Come on," Carrie whispered. "I have a better idea."

She took her hand and led her to the farthest corner of the little hallway. "Is this better?"

"Yes, much."

With her hand under Moni's chin, Carrie lifted her face upward. "I've been wanting to do this all evening," she said, kissing her strong and full. Their bodies came together as Moni returned the kiss. Held securely in Carrie's embrace, her body softened and her lips yielded to desire. The intensity of their kisses deepened and became passionate. Moni's body responded with a tremendous rush of heat and a demand not easily overridden.

When voices from the other room drew nearer the hallway, Moni eased her lips from Carrie's and pressed the side of her head to her cheek. The arms loosened around her. "I guess people are getting ready to leave," Moni said quietly.

"And you're in the hallway making out with me," Carrie said, her lips making their way down Moni's neck. "Is that a problem?"

"Shouldn't we be polite and say good night?"

Her sigh muffled into the hair at Moni's temple. "Politeness is not what I'm feeling."

With a reluctant but smiling Carrie next to her, Moni bid cordial good-byes as the women left. Carrie would be staying the night and driving back tomorrow. When the last couple rose to leave and Gina went after their jackets, Moni called after her. "Get mine, too, Gina."

But Carrie took her hand. "Don't leave yet."
Moni looked into pleading blue eyes and sat down.

"Pillows, blankets, and privacy," smiled Dedra, delivering her offering on the end of the couch. Gina embraced her affectionately, obviously relieved that Dedra had behaved herself all night. *Of course*, Moni thought, *she's been too busy playing cupid*.

"Once that bedroom door shuts, we're in for the night," Gina said with a mischievous grin.

"I'll see you tomorrow," Carrie laughed, leaning back on the couch.

"Good night," Moni called after them.

Carrie relaxed against the back of the couch, then turned to look at Moni. "Hmm, where was it we left off?"

Moni leaned over her. When their lips met, Carrie wasted no time. She caressed the silky material of Moni's blouse, her hands thoroughly covering her back and sides. She pressed open Moni's lips. The heat began to build again. Moni opened her mouth wider, giving permission, letting her in. Carrie's hand, now firmly caressing the inside of her thigh, intensified the heat and wetness. And as her hand moved even higher, Moni knew she would let Carrie make love to her tonight.

Smoothly and effortlessly, Carrie embraced her again, leaning her back against the pillows. She kissed Moni's neck more aggressively and unbuttoned her blouse. Her desire was obvious. Moni pulled the blouse from Carrie's slacks and with her fingers followed the telltale flow of perspiration along the hollow of her spine. A large, strong hand covered Moni's breast, while insistent lips left a wet trail across her chest. Moni shifted her hips, giving teasing fingers access to her pants closure.

But the moan that should have accompanied the feel of her zipper opening to the touch of a lover's hand didn't come. And the lips that had stirred the coals of desire now pressed the flesh of her breast futilely. The heat of her body had suddenly vaporized into a cold sweat. Desire had vanished. In its place was an eerie emptiness. Moni closed her eyes and floated to the ceiling. She saw herself lying there on the couch, a woman ardently caressing the shell she'd left behind.

She saw Carrie look up into her face and heard her words. "Are you crying?" It was only then that she felt the tears wetting her cheeks, her hair, and rolling into her ear. "What's wrong?" she heard.

"I don't know," Moni whispered, covering her eyes. "I'm sorry."

Carrie leaned her head back against the couch. "Jesus, Moni," she said, taking a deep breath. "I thought you wanted this as much as I did."

The room was still and uncomfortably silent. Moni heard herself say the words, just above a whisper. "So did I."

Carrie took two more deep breaths, letting them out slowly. "Are we cheating on someone here?"

"No." *How do I possibly explain this? I can't even make sense of it myself. If I had only followed my first instinct, I wouldn't have done this to her.* "I'm sorry, Carrie." Tears still flowed from her covered eyes. She was so embarrassed; she couldn't bear to look at her.

"There's someone else?"

The buttons of her blouse were being rebuttoned. *No, and there probably won't be.* But she nodded anyway. She just wanted to be home.

Carrie stood, took Moni's hands, and pulled her to her feet. "If she loved you, Moni, she'd be here instead of me." She wiped the remnants of tears from Moni's cheeks. "It's okay," Carrie said softly. "I'll drive you home."

"Are you going to be all right?" Carrie asked as Moni started out the car door.

"I'm embarrassed," she said with an attempt to smile. "I don't want you to think I'm a head case."

"I don't." She waited for Moni's reluctant eyes. "I do think it's a shame, though." She took Moni's hand and placed a piece of paper in her palm. "Here's my number. Maybe you'll feel like calling me later."

Maybe. Or, more likely, I'll never put myself or anyone else in such an uncomfortable position again. "Thanks for bringing me home."

SEVEN

Gazing out of the second-story window, Moni watched the lazy strides of spring carry the students over the lawns and sidewalks of campus. She was only half listening to the speech being given. Hers was over, having been presented on Tuesday, leaving her relaxed and admittedly a little complacent. Yet not so much so that she could ignore the scrutiny of Katherine Cunningham. *Katherine* to Moni's unspoken thoughts. She was sitting only two seats up with her back to the windows, watching the class as well as the speaker. Moni changed her focus to the young man with the bad complexion and the much improved speaking skills. One of Katherine's minor miracles.

Moni could count herself among Ms. Cunningham's works of wonder. How she had dreaded taking this speech class, putting it off until the final session of her junior year. Now it was nearly over and probably the most valuable class she had taken. In one semester the shy detachment that had hidden so many fears had been transformed into a creative self-confidence. She spoke now without fear of criticism or ridicule. And while this transformation was taking place there was a belief, planted and nurtured, that what she had to say was worthy of being listened to.

How one instructor could have been so effective was remarkable. With a manner as natural as falling leaves in autumn, Katherine Cunningham simply changed fear into laughter, laughter that said "Just knowing you have the same fears makes me feel so much better." Before they knew it, students were offering support to each other, words of encouragement, smiles of understanding. They realized they all had to go through the same process, and doing it together made it much more comfortable. The inevitable result was not only good speaking skills but mutual respect as well. And they had gotten there without one word of criticism. It seemed almost too simple. To give the credit to good teaching methods would be a disservice to the woman who mastered them. It wasn't so much the methods, Moni realized, as it was how they were applied. Katherine would look into their eyes and smile, and suddenly the young men became handsome and the women felt beautiful.

It was nothing tangible, only a feeling. But there was magic in the power it gave, and in the power she had given them to speak to the world.

Moni's eyes rested again on the woman who had intrigued her from the first day of class. Without her knowing it, Katherine Cunningham had become an unplanned but refreshing interlude to a dull, lonely year. Moni's much needed diversion from loneliness. At first she had intentionally brought the stunning English transplant into the empty silences late at night, filling the times when she felt most alone with the charm of her accent and the lilt of her laughter. Gradually, though, she found Katherine filling unexpected thoughts during her study breaks and during the long walks across campus, popping into Moni's life outside of class without warning. She didn't know how long she'd been reacting to everything as if Katherine were standing right next to her; she'd only realized it last week. A regression to younger years and her infatuations with older women, Moni admitted. She'd even kept a copy of a practice run of a sixty-second descriptive assignment, one never intended to be given, in the back of her notebook. Regression this bad had to be kept to herself.

Katherine Cunningham:
In the Artist's Eye

The artist matches lines with the woman in her sights. Quick composite lines sweep broadly over shoulders, drop sleekly down slender arms, glide over narrow hips. Long lines of leg define their statuesque pose, and tease the eyes into tracing them again.

Poses move in natural grace from page to

page through the artist's pad. The characteristic lean against the front of the desk then changes to a standing recital from an open book held high in one hand. And the artist takes a closer look.

She pays special attention to subtle shading below prominent cheekbones, along the gentle slope of a narrow nose. And draws the delicate lines that define the perfect mouth.

Still, the artist searches for the magic that is her art, to capture a glimpse of the soul. Whispering its essence on the curve of her neck, and the tilt of her head, radiating through her eyes. What is it the artist sees, Katherine Cunningham?

"Tuesday will be our last class meeting," she was saying, raising Moni from her trance. "We will hear our last two speeches. Then I'll ask for some feedback from you on how beneficial you thought the class was, and collect your evaluation of my presentation. And that'll be it. You will have made it through your most dreaded class." Ms. Cunningham raised her hands to the side and flashed a bright white smile that radiated to the depths of Moni's soul.

The class applauded and began to disperse. And it was over. The class no one wanted to take — the one Moni wanted never to end. Beginning Wednesday, Katherine Cunningham must become only a wonderful memory.

EIGHT

As usual, the summer was too short. The time had been divided between taking eight credit hours of classes and teaching swimming for the recreation department. There'd been very little time for anything else. But busy did not negate loneliness. A weekend here and there with family could only do so much. The summer session had come and gone, and so had many acquaintances. Friends had separated and moved away. It wasn't the same now when she visited home.

Dedra, too, had graduated, taking a job on the other side of the state. Jean was all she had left. She hoped she understood how much her friendship was appreciated.

Classes would begin this week, but not before Moni met with the head of the women's physical education department. Like all university students, she was required to fulfill two credit hours of swimming. But when they found that she'd been teaching aquatics for four years, they tested her out of all the classes and decided to put her to work. She knew only that she'd be assisting a sub in covering the teaching assignment of an instructor out on emergency medical leave. It was all she needed to know, along with the fact that she'd be paid for all time beyond her required credits.

The sound of women's laughter drifted into the hallway as Moni neared Dr. Young's office. The gentler sounds had a strangely familiar lilt. Rounding the corner of the office, she was shocked to see Katherine Cunningham talking with Dr. Young.

"Moni, come in," Dr. Young said, still laughing. "This is Katherine Cunningham. The English department graciously loaned her to us when we found we had no qualified subs left. You'll be helping her teach the two intermediate classes."

"Hi, Moni," Katherine greeted her, then redirected her attention to Dr. Young, "Moni took a speech class from me . . . It's good to see you again."

"It's good to see you." *No, it's wonderful. It's wonderful to see you. You just keep right on smiling those stabs of electricity straight through my heart all semester*, Moni smiled.

"Let me acquaint you two a little bit, and then

you should probably find some time to talk over how you want to handle your teaching assignment together," Dr. Young was saying. "Katherine's background includes six years as waterfront director at a large private camp in Connecticut. A lot of organizational and supervisory experience, plus enough teaching to keep her credentials current. Does that sum things up pretty well?

"Very well," Katherine replied.

"And, Moni, during the past four years you've taught swimming to every age group that exists, I see." Dr. Young raised her eyebrows.

Moni smiled through her blush. "Tiny tots to senior sorts."

"Yes. And I observed your demonstration skills when we tested you out of classes . . . Katherine, you should not hesitate to have Moni demonstrate any skill you think is needed. And, Moni, don't be afraid to speak up and teach the way you know works best. I am very grateful, and happy, to have you both helping us out here. You saved us from having to cancel a class. Remember, my office is always open, and I expect you to pop in here anytime you have a question . . . or if you just want to visit," Dr. Young concluded.

"Thank you. You've made me feel quite welcome already," Katherine said as she stood.

"I really appreciate this opportunity," Moni said, shaking Dr. Young's hand.

"How about if we hit the ole union for lunch and talk things over," Katherine offered. "Do you have time right now?"

"Yes, I do. My classes don't start until tomorrow."

"Why do you want to teach, Moni?" Katherine asked from across a small table.

Being suddenly alone with this woman was replacing the comfort Moni normally felt with those older than herself with an unsettling nervousness. She attempted to mask it with methods Katherine herself had taught her. Slow, controlled breaths — pause before you speak. "The first time I was asked that question, I was sure my reasons had everything to do with education being more secure than the career of an artist . . ." She chased the ice cubes around her glass with the tip of her straw. "Now I think it has more to do with respect."

"Teaching is not a highly respected profession in the States, you know."

"Yes, I know. That's what makes my reasoning so ironic." She hesitated, wondering how concisely she could condense years of thought.

"I hope you don't mind my asking. I thought if we got to know each other a little, it would make working together more comfortable."

"Oh, you're right," replied Moni, looking close up for the first time into stunningly beautiful light brown eyes. "I'm trying to give you the *Reader's Digest* version," she said over the electrical shock shooting through her chest. "And I'm not looking for sympathy by my answer; I'm only trying to be honest."

"Understood."

"I was never accepted by my peers growing up. As hard as I tried, I didn't fit in, and they refused to accept me as I was. I always felt too plain, too poor, too shy. It didn't matter how much it hurt me. In fact, they seemed to revel in my pain. All I wanted was for them to give me a chance. They never did . . ." Moni looked from the glass she'd been rolling between her palms into eyes riveted on her own. "Maybe I can teach their children to respect others' feelings."

"Through art."

"Through expression . . . and respecting expression. It takes a certain amount of courage to express yourself visually . . . and to let others see it. It's humbling for some, empowering for others."

"A most noble revenge if ever I heard one." She lifted her glass in a toast. "To the diversity of young minds" — she tilted her head — "and the courage to express."

Moni lifted her glass and smiled. "And to summers off to draw."

"Aha!"

NINE

For six weeks they worked together on a first-name basis, equally sharing the teaching of skills and dividing the class for practice time. Decisions were made jointly, respect shown mutually. The scenario was one that Moni could not have imagined even in her most creative fantasies. She marveled at what the shy little girl of eight years ago would have thought had she been able to see the future.

As she waited at the table for Katherine, she wondered about the frequent lunches. In the beginning the meetings were essential to working smoothly together. They had evolved, however, into casual get-togethers. And although she would never wish it away, she questioned why Katherine spent this time with her. She also found herself questioning her original assumption that Katherine was straight. Often she tried to visualize the kind of men Katherine might be attracted to. Yet even with the absence of a ring, she thought it strange that Katherine had only mentioned one man, David Shanks. "A wonderfully unorthodox teacher who dares to give Shakespeare's characters a regular seat in his classroom. Not an easy thing to pull off successfully," Katherine told her. "An enjoyable man, but for his disturbingly unchecked libido." And that was it. Not a word about dating in all these weeks. It seemed strange only because Katherine was comfortable talking about so many other things. Maybe her private life was indeed too private. There were few who would be as open as Jean, and fewer whom she had known so long . . . Of course, there was always the possibility that she was gay. A wonderfully intriguing thought.

"You're a sweet woman, Moni Matteson," Katherine said, her customary thank you for having iced tea waiting for her. She glided around Moni's chair, leaving the scent of her perfume on the stirred air, and eased gracefully into the seat across the table. "I'm sorry I'm late. I've been rushing since the beginning of the semester, it seems," she said, neatly arranging a pile of folders. "I've been so concerned with keeping one step ahead, I haven't taken time to say things I've intended." She stopped and looked at Moni. "Like how much I like your hair short" — she smiled — "and highlighted like that."

Moni marveled at how a compliment from this woman could do such physical things to her. "This is drastic for me . . . no chance of turning back. But being in the water every day, I should have done it years ago."

"And, before I forget," Katherine continued, "I wanted to tell you that I'm glad we decided to let the synchronized group practice during our class. I don't mind taking your group while you help them. It's working out fine." She stopped alphabetizing folders and looked up. "You've dramatically improved the on-deck moves before their entry. Where did you learn to move like that?" she asked, with a grin much too private, much too inviting.

Not sure how to respond, Moni kept her answer brief. "They're just a combination of dance moves."

"I think it's more in *how* you do them."

"I had a good teacher."

"Yes, you did," she replied, holding her gaze just long enough for Moni to blush through her summer tan. It seemed to amuse Katherine. Moni pulled her eyes away and nibbled her chicken salad.

"Speaking of teachers," Katherine continued. "Despite the closeness in age, you command a lot of respect from your students. Just knowing your stuff isn't enough, Moni. You have a gift."

"Maybe." She pushed a glasslike cube to the bottom of the glass and watched it fight its way to the surface. "But I owe a lot to another good teacher." How to maintain sophistication with a red blush all over her face was beyond her. "I've wanted to tell you how much I respect you . . ."

"Moni, I already know how you feel." Moni looked

up at her in surprise. Katherine laughed softly. "I kept your evaluation from speech class separate, so I'd know what you thought. You said such nice things."

"Why did you want to know what *I* thought?"

"Curiosity, I suppose. Does it bother you?"

Moni was trying to remember what all she had written on the evaluation. "I don't know. I never thought you'd know who wrote it, so I said things I'd be too embarrassed to say to your face."

Katherine waited for Moni to look at her. "You know what I wish you would do? I wish you would talk to me when we're alone with the same confidence you have with your students."

"I'm not sure how to act around you," Moni admitted between consciously controlled breaths. The gaze from the light brown eyes seemed to draw her close. "I find myself looking for the line I'm not supposed to cross."

"When I figure out where it should be, I'll let you know." She smiled. "Until then, just be yourself around me."

"I've been trying to do just that."

Katherine smiled even more. "Whenever you find you're having trouble, remember that I'm just a woman, Moni — with abilities you can count on one hand, and faults that would undoubtedly take two. I suspect you have abilities I haven't even seen yet, and far fewer faults."

"*That* I wouldn't bet on . . . you may not like what you see."

"No, *that* you shouldn't bet on."

Despite her heart's attempt to leave her chest, she

58

managed, "I can be a real smart-ass — and downright cynical."

"Really," Katherine replied, gathering her things and rising. "And should that break my heart?"

TEN

For days, she had tried to find time to get to the library. Tonight she didn't care how tired she was or how late it got, she was going to satisfy her curiosity. Moni headed straight for the computer and immediately accessed the catalogue. It occurred to her after their last lunch together, that instructors at the university level are expected to be published within a certain length of time. How long a time she didn't know, but Katherine had taught at the university for three years. And her writing could be anything from a dissertation on public speaking techniques to a novel about a modern-day Lolita. But if one is good at reading between the lines, insights into Katherine could be gained from whatever she had written.

Cunningham ... Katherine. There it was. And not just one title, but two. "Yes, Miss Katherine," she said out loud. "You're going to talk to me tonight." Moni quickly found the two small poetry books and excitedly settled into a secluded nook. Checking the publishing dates, she decided to read the earlier one first. It didn't guarantee chronological accuracy, but the chances were better.

Slowly she read each poem, trying to relate each to what it might be saying about Katherine's personal life. The poems spoke of love and passion, many of them causing her to blush and perspire, even in her privacy. Flipping back through the pages, unwilling to go on yet, she read them again. Then back again, to one that sent a shot through her chest each time she read it.

> *Touch me with your passion*
> *fill me with your love.*
> *Make me know your words are true*
> *and told to me alone.*

> *I'll let you touch my heart*
> *expose it to you whole.*
> *And let you claim my body*
> *knowing you'll take my soul.*

Leaning back in her chair, she tried to visualize Katherine, glowing with the passion of love and welcoming a lover to her bed. The vision was so sensual it was almost too embarrassing to hold, yet she made herself ask the questions. *Who had she fallen in love with? It was years ago, but had it been a man or a woman?* There had not been one indication of gender. *So did omission make it obvious?*

Maybe the second book . . . She quickly opened it to the first poem, and slowly again read straight through. The tone was very different from the first. The words were filled with pain and told of love threatened or lost. Her anguish touched Moni's heart.

Night
Quiet, dark.
Thoughts so intense,
Fears so real.
Sadness comes to tears,
Love to pain.
Alone
I wait.
Feelings exposed.
No help
From the night.
Will emptiness win?

Moni leaned forward, resting her forehead in the palm of one hand. *Katherine with her private pain, her secret life. What is it about her that makes me need to know? What makes this heart search for an answer that logic speaks soundly against? And what do I know now? That Katherine is an emotional, deeply passionate woman. That she's known pain and loneliness . . . and love. That I don't know if her life now is happy and fulfilled. That I care if it is.*

Yet happy or not, gay or not, common sense will win in the end. And there will be no more unbridled curiosity, or endearing thoughts. They will remain tucked away, deep in the deepest corner of my soul, where all precious things are kept. For there is one thing I do know for sure . . . I must not fall in love with this woman.

ELEVEN

The lights of the city and passing traffic twinkled through the raindrops running down the library window. The little room on the second floor of the old city library was Moni's own private solace. She stood watching the silent city. It was dark now. She'd been drawing for a couple of hours. A walk downstairs to stretch her legs, and a drink of water, and she would probably be good for another hour or so.

Despite promises to the contrary, most of the evening had been spent thinking of Katherine. Even now, at the fountain, she could smell her perfume.

Either her senses were playing tricks on her or someone else was teasing her. Taking a deep breath, she
strolled slowly back toward the stairs.

"Moni."

She turned quickly at the sound of her name, and
there in the middle of the hall, arms full of books,
was Katherine.

"Working late, are you?" She smiled.

Unable to hide her pleasure, Moni returned an
even bigger smile. "Yes, trying to finish a drawing.
Here, let me take some of those," she said, relieving
Katherine of half the stack. With a raise of an eyebrow she asked, "Would you care to join me in my
private room?"

"Lead on," Katherine laughed.

"I come here a lot," Moni explained, entering the
small room. "Especially when my roommates have
people over. There's never anyone here this late." She
placed the books on the other side of the table. "I love
the architecture of this building, the marble, these
heavy wooden tables. I feel comfortable here."

"Yes. I come here in the evenings instead of the
university library. And now I know why I've never
seen you here. You've found the perfect hideaway."
Her eyes were surveying the nearly finished nude.
"She's beautiful. Who is she?"

"My favorite Michelangelo statue. She's called
Dawn."

"She looks so supple — almost warm. It's as
though you've given her life."

"She was commissioned to sit at the tomb of
Lorenzo de' Medici. *Night*, the male, sits on the other
side. There's been a lot of symbolism attached to her
through the years, a reawakening, the beginning of

65

life, the life after darkness. I had this need to put her on paper, to . . . recreate her . . . bring her to life? I don't know."

"Self-analysis? Should I read anything into this?"

"I don't know if it's worth the effort."

"Might tell me something about the real Moni Matteson."

"What you see is —"

"Huh-uh. I don't buy it."

Moni smiled. *Ridiculous game to play with this woman.* "Okay. Read whatever you wish. But I've done some reading of my own. *Impassioned Heart. Songs of Silence?*" Moni smiled at the surprise on Katherine's face. "No symbolism there — just straight-out raw emotion. It surprised me."

"What *did* you expect?"

"I don't know," Moni laughed. "Symbolism."

Katherine offered a gentle, almost private laugh and moved to her side of the table. The discussion, evidently, had gone as far as she wanted it to go.

Organizing her books, she began working quietly, while Moni began a discreet but diligent study. Katherine in an oversize sweatshirt and a pair of jeans, a fascinating contradiction in beauty. Not the sleek sophistication of formfitting suits and heels or the sensuality of naked skin exposed in a bathing suit. Tonight she looked less ominous, a beautiful coed with a vulnerability that invited teasing and cuddling . . . and loving.

Dammit, Moni! Why don't you sit here and day-dream right in front of her? While you're at it, why don't you admit you're falling in love with her? Go ahead, make a fool out of yourself. Fantasy is safe haven for fools.

Katherine looked up to change books, and Moni quickly refocused on her drawing. *Be grateful she can't read your silly mind, dream girl.* After as many uncounted moments as she could stand, she chanced another look and found Katherine watching her. This time she didn't look away, and neither did Katherine. Sharp little sensations were darting through her, sent there by the mysterious brown eyes. Maybe Katherine wasn't concentrating any better than she was. With only a slight smile, Moni forced her attention away from her chance to find out. *Daydreams don't require bravery.*

A while later, Moni got up and walked to the window. It was getting late. She could hear Katherine beginning to put her papers in order.

"I didn't realize what time it was," she said.

Moni turned toward the table as Katherine stacked the books near the edge. "I'll help you with those," she offered, reaching forward. Just then the top book tumbled toward the floor, and both women reached for it at the same time. As they lunged forward, Moni's head brushed the side of Katherine's face and shoulder. "I'm sorry," Moni said, picking up the book.

Katherine grasped Moni's hand. Neither of them moved as Katherine spoke. "Don't be," she said, as Moni dared a look up at the face only inches from her own. Katherine squeezed her hand, while her eyes bore so deeply into Moni's that it seemed they knew every secret. The definitive move, as clear as fine crystal, that stopped Moni in a breathless trance and said what she had not even dared to dream. Not only was Katherine Cunningham gay — she was attracted. Moni's heart throbbed mercilessly as Katherine's fingertips gently touched her cheek. Then without a word, she pulled her eyes from Moni's and stood.

Moni finally found her breath, and despite feeling as if she'd just finished a hundred lengths of the pool, she stood and replaced the book. Her eyes remained on Katherine as she gathered the books in her arms.

"Good night, Moni." Without a glance she left the room — and left Moni to snap herself out of what was no longer a daydream.

TWELVE

"Moni, will you douse the lights?" Katherine asked, hitting the play button on the videocassette player. A click of the switch darkened the little room, except for the light coming from the large glass window looking out to the pool. She was grateful that Katherine liked the idea of the water safety video. It provided a welcome break from two hectic weeks. Major assignments all due at the same time, she decided, was sick, egotistical warfare between college instructors. Whoever received the largest return on their demand must be most important in the hierarchy. *Sure*. And maybe it had been merciful that Katherine had made no indication that there'd been even the slightest glitch in their "normal" professional/social relationship. *Thank you very much.* So much to be grateful for, she mused. And she wouldn't even have to get wet today. She smoothed a foreign thread from her slacks, rolled it into a ball, and leaned against the glass to watch the swimmers in the pool.

Rick Gilbert's beginning class occupied the shallow end of the pool. Moni watched the cocky young instructor standing at the end of the pool with his arms crossed. She didn't like him much, partly because he was always coming on to Katherine and partly because he was a terrible teacher. He was lazy, arrogant and, in a pool, potentially dangerous.

The proof had emerged more than once over the semester. A large male student, with very weak technique, had often wandered close to the deeper water in the middle of the pool. Each time Rick had loudly called him back but made no other attempt to solve the problem. There were methods, fairly simple ones, that would help him as well as minimize the danger. Moni knew them from experience. Rick, however, seemed to have no clue. So after the third incident, Moni began coming in a few minutes early and putting out a buoy line. It wouldn't solve the problem, but it would get the swimmer's attention. Out of concern for the student, she even asked Katherine to take a couple of suggestions down to Rick.

Although not crazy about the idea, Katherine agreed the suggestions were good ones: assigning the student the lane next to the end of the pool, and making him keep eye contact with a whistle Rick carried while he walked the end. But Rick Gilbert did not take suggestions readily. Or maybe he didn't like them coming from a woman. Whatever his reason, the situation remained the same, and Moni tried to ignore things after that.

Moni's eyes left the familiar images on the screen to acknowledge the attentiveness of the students, to move swiftly past Katherine sitting near the far wall, and to glance casually into the pool area. Immediately she noticed the weak, jerky freestyle of the wandering student curving slowly away from shallow water. She stood and searched for Rick, finally finding him talking with a student near his office. He didn't see the swimmer. Her eyes quickly darted back to the water — no buoy line. The swimmer had crossed the shallow end and was still going. Moni bolted to the door, which alerted Katherine and the class. Looking out, Katherine saw the urgency of the situation and started after Moni. They ran around the end of the pool and started down the other side. Moni knew that to yell at him now would certainly panic the swimmer, right in the middle of the deep end. Her hope was that he wouldn't look until he was close enough to the side that she could assist him.

Meanwhile, their movement had also alerted Rick Gilbert, and despite her attempts to wave him off, he dove into the water. The situation had just become even more dangerous. "Stupid shit," Moni said aloud. "*Never* go in till you have to."

"I'm right behind you," Katherine said, grabbing the pole from the wall.

The hope that the swimmer would reach the side before opening his eyes was erased almost immediately. Probably feeling the swimmer behind him, he raised his head. And just as Moni knew would happen, he panicked. Immediately she yelled to Rick, "Stay back. Stay back! Let us get him with the pole."

"We're right here. You're all right," Katherine was calling. "We'll pull you in." She tried to maneuver the hook around the thick, bobbing waist. But heavy arms thrashing wildly and barely keeping his head above water, made it difficult.

"I almost had him."

"It's okay," Moni encouraged. "It'll be easier as he tires. There's plenty of time."

But unfortunately, panic wasn't reserved for the student. Rick Gilbert also panicked, and despite Moni yelling no over and over, he went for the swimmer.

She shouted, "Too close!" But Moni's warning echoed from the walls and drowned in the churning water.

Rick's position was poor, putting him in reach of the swimmer who, at this point, was totally irrational. Seeing Rick as merely a large buoy, he grabbed and climbed. The struggle was on. Rick was no physical match for the much larger, heavier student who was panicking for air. They both went under. Moni could see the student clutching Rick's head desperately to his chest, and even Rick's best kicking efforts couldn't bring their heads up.

"Shit. He's a sinker," she said, quickly stripping off her slacks. "He'll take them to the bottom."

Before Katherine could respond, Moni was in the water headed for the sinking, struggling bodies. Her dive took her near the bottom before she reached the pair and grabbed the larger man's chin from behind with both hands. Explosively she rammed her foot against Rick's shoulder. The bodies slipped apart.

She kicked hard to move the heavy student. If she could only get them far enough apart before she had to go for air. Harder and harder she kicked. She let out more air to relieve the pressure in her chest, but it was beginning to hurt. Then just as she was about to let go, Moni saw the surface.

Bursting out of the water, she gulped air as if it would be her last, and his weight pulled her under again. With the oxygen renewing her strength, she gave two more strong kicks and cleared both their heads above the surface. He gulped and choked and gulped again, and suddenly his thrashing stopped. Moni kicked for the side, breathing only after each kick while his weight forced her under between kicks.

With his efforts concentrated on gasping for air and coughing now, he became almost passive for the last few feet to the side. Katherine reached down, grabbed his arm, and pulled him to the edge.

Moni, bright red and thoroughly exhausted, leaned her head back on the water and took a deep breath. The amount of air made her dizzy. She returned to the side, stretched her arms across the pool's edge, and rested her head. Katherine and Rick dragged the student from the water.

"Dammit, Mike," goaded Rick. "When are you gonna lose some weight? You're dangerous."

Moni turned her head away in an attempt to control what she wanted to say so badly. *How do assholes like you get positions like this?* Arrogance and stupidity were two things she had no tolerance for anymore. And right now, she was too mad to even try to figure out which he was.

"Nice job, Moni," came the wonderful voice that began instantly cleansing her anger. "Are you all right?" Katherine asked.

"Yeah, just tired," she answered, slipping back into the water. "I'll use the ladder."

Shaky from the adrenaline and her efforts, Moni pulled herself up the steps. The student was resting against the wall, Rick kneeling in front of him. "You're welcome, Mr. Gilbert," Moni said, only half controlling her flaring anger. Katherine, within earshot, approached and touched her wet head reassuringly. "Sorry," Moni apologized.

"Come on, we'll find you some dry clothes," Katherine offered, carrying Moni's slacks. "And I have to find out if I'm supposed to fill out some kind of report."

Moni leaned her head back into the shower spray. The warmth cascaded down her body while thousands of tiny beads began to relax the tensed muscles and gently massage away the remaining anger. She took a deep breath of steamy air. No doubt about it, she was going to hurt tomorrow.

"Moni, I've got a sweatshirt here for you. I'm drying your underwear under the hair dryer," Katherine called through the door.

* * * * *

When she finally emerged from the bathroom, Moni found Katherine finishing a report.

"I did have to fill one out," she said, looking up. "And Dr. Young would like to thank the heroine personally." She hesitated before adding, "You *were* mag- nificent, Moni."

Despite the look she just received sending a lightning bolt through her chest, Moni dragged her toe across the floor. "Aw shucks. It was nothin' any red-blooded American . . . it was nothing."

"Really," Katherine laughed. "I'll bet your muscles call you a liar tomorrow. Come on."

Even twenty minutes of complimentary conversation with Dr. Young couldn't make her feel what Katherine had with only three words: "You were magnificent." Without trying, without even thinking, Moni had clearly impressed her. Maybe she shouldn't be so upset with Rick Gilbert after all. She smiled to herself as she and Katherine found a seat in a small restaurant off campus. Katherine's insistence on taking her to lunch couldn't be resisted. Besides, it was a good enough excuse for a date, wasn't it?

Katherine began with more compliments. "Well, Ms. Matteson, you not only know your stuff; you're quite good under pressure."

"That was automatic mode. I'm really not conscious of making decisions. The compliment should go to the teacher who trained me."

"Then my hat's off to . . ."

"Jean Kesh . . . fine teacher, and a good friend."

"So, you *usually* make friends out of your teachers." Katherine grinned that grin, the one that said *I suspect I already know the answer to that, and more.*

"Actually, no. It depends on where the line is drawn." Jean's had been clearly drawn just past friendship. *Your line, dear Katherine, escapes me.* Still no help from Katherine. "Jean was a friend before she was my teacher. She remained a friend even after tolerating my childhood." Moni smiled.

After a brief interruption to order, their conversation naturally returned to the event of the day. They agreed that Rick Gilbert fit perfectly into the macho-shithead category and aptly owed the remainder of his probably worthless life to what he obviously considered a weaker and less intelligent being. *That*, they figured, would be embarrassment enough for him. Plus, by tomorrow everyone on campus will have heard about it, to say nothing of the embarrassment he faced from the department's inquiry. No, an apology, or even a thank you, wasn't necessary. Moni's anger was conquered.

With a little prompting Moni shared four other times she had saved someone from the water, while Katherine listened intently. Then, an unexpected bonus. Just as naturally as she would discuss the day's weather, Katherine began talking about the years she spent at her friend's waterfront camp in Connecticut. *All those years in one place, one person ... and she was writing during that time.* The pieces began falling into place. There was a sadness, too, in her eyes, in her voice. She tried to hide it, but her eyes stared past Moni's with a vacant reminiscence. The corners of her mouth stopped short of even the gentlest crease of her laugh lines.

Moni watched her with growing empathy. If it were

only possible, she would take away the sadness in an instant. If only she knew how, she would replace the loneliness. She would fill the moments of doubt with hope, change the sadness to laughter, and heal the emotional wounds with a salve of understanding. The very same things Katherine had begun to do for her. But theirs was a relationship that danced in the shadows of friendship, holding out hope of ecstatic happiness while promising total devastation. And like all dances it was destined to end.

She watched Katherine finish the last of her salad. "Have you written anything recently?" Moni asked.

"A few relatively boring articles for our quarterly. Only a couple of inspired pieces. Not enough to publish. I've found I'm not a stop-and-smell-the-roses type of poet. Makes me realize how wise my decision was to teach." Katherine lowered her eyes and set her dish aside. "Passion alone can't sustain life . . . nor can a career, I've found."

It was a recognizable need for Moni now: tapping in to this woman's intellect, into her soul. Tasting it had only awakened a deeper thirst. "What does?" she asked.

"The answer is as old as the human race" — she tilted her head — "as obvious as Romeo and Juliet . . . as pure as Naomi and Ruth. For me . . . Here, do something with me." She reached into her purse and produced a tablet and two pens. Handing Moni a piece of paper she said, "I'll ask some questions and we'll write our answers, then exchange them."

The tactic was obvious. Written answers would be uncompromised by the other's responses. Moni smiled to herself. "Teachers never quit giving tests, do they?"

"Come on, be a sport," Katherine pleaded.

"I'm only kidding. What's the question?"

Katherine returned the smile, an appreciation of the young woman who made her smile from the inside out. "Okay," she said. "First question. Is happiness a state of being, or a state of mind?"

Neither of them hesitated long before writing her answer.

"Ready?" she asked, receiving a nod from Moni. "Okay, let's see . . . If a hundred people looked at an object, and ninety-nine said it was red and I said it was blue — what color is it?"

Moni recorded a thoughtful answer, *To ninety-nine it is red. To one it is blue.* "Next?"

"Hmm. Let's say it's only possible for you to have one of the following in your life: to have enough money to buy everything you ever wanted, to be historically famous and respected for your work, or to be in love with someone who loves you more than anything on earth. Money, fame, or love — and only the first two guaranteed to last a lifetime. Which would you choose?"

Moni quickly wrote something on her paper and looked up.

"That was fast."

"It was an easy question."

"Uh-huh," grinned Katherine, writing down her answer. "Last question: Is it possible to enjoy good sex without being in love?"

The question caught Moni completely off guard. The surprise must have shown on her face.

"I'm sorry. If you think that was out of line, you don't have to answer it."

"No." Moni relaxed a little. "You asked it. I'll answer it." She acknowledged Katherine's grin as confirmation that this test was beyond the realm of curiosity, and wrote her answer. Also an easy one. Carrie had been convincing proof.

She took the paper Katherine folded over her fingers, and slid her own across the table. She read in silence, then watched Katherine fold the paper in half and smile. "So now what do you know?" Moni asked.

"The same thing you know. That each of us would give up virtually everything for a chance at real love . . . despite how many people thought it was wrong."

Moni stared in amazement at the ease by which she had been analyzed. "Give this test often, do you?"

"Oh, no." Katherine frowned. "Totally impromptu. Right off the top of my head."

Moni stifled a smile. "Mmm, I see." She nodded. "Okay, smarty, I have a question for *you*." Katherine rested her chin on clasped hands and waited. "If forever can't be identified by its end, and you don't know when it began, how do you know it exists?"

It was Katherine's turn to be impressed — by a young woman with such an old soul. "I think you may have found the question with no answer."

THIRTEEN

Jean's soft, airy voice could never be mistaken for anyone else's. "Hello?"

Nor could Moni's after all this time. "Are you busy?"

"No, and even if I were, I'd expect you to come over. If I find that you've been in town and didn't call, I'll be terribly hurt."

"I'll help you with whatever you're doing. Is this Ken's Saturday to work?"

"Yes. You'll have to stay for dinner if you want to see him."

"Actually, I'd like to talk with you alone."

"Is everything all right?"

"I'm in need of a little advice. See you in fifteen minutes."

Moni pulled a large blue towel from the basket and folded it in thirds, then in half the way Jean liked it. *It should be easier than this. I've trusted Jean with so many things. What makes this so hard? The one thing I've never been able to tell her. How many times have I been this close and chickened out? And now there is so much more involved. Maybe a student just shouldn't tell a teacher that she is in love with another teacher, friend or no friend.*

"How's the swim show coming?" Jean asked, plopping another basket of freshly dried laundry onto the couch.

"I could use some help on the All-American number. Something isn't working."

"Is that what you needed advice on?"

"Uh-huh."

"I'm glad it's nothing serious. You had me worried." Jean picked up the pile of Ken's folded T-shirts and placed them back in the basket. "You never told me what happened to the teacher of the student you pulled out of the pool."

"Not much to tell. He got a departmental reprimand. I doubt he was even embarrassed. Never even thanked me. But I didn't really expect him to."

"I'd say he's pretty lucky. Negligence at that level is inexcusable."

"Well, that was my excitement for the semester. How about you?"

Jean finished folding the peach set of towels with a final pat. "Only our monthly argument over starting a family. Should I be grateful?"

Moni met her eyes with the understanding she knew Jean expected. "Not ready for Pampers, car seats, and Molly and her dolly?"

Jean forced a smile. "I believe a mother should be with her babies when they're young. I can't do that right now. Maybe it would be different if I didn't love teaching so much."

"You're feeling guilty."

"Ken would make a wonderful father. It isn't fair to him."

"And it wouldn't be fair for you to bear a child out of guilt."

Jean made another attempt to smile. "I guess we're fated to argue, until one of us gives in . . . or we divorce."

Moni snatched the last towel from Jean's hands. "Why don't you come spend the weekend on campus with me during next month's row?"

"And check out the campus color?"

The look on Moni's face was a combination of mock surprise and mild disgust. "Right. And let you leap from the frying pan into the fire? I think not."

Jean's mood had lightened into a mischievous giggle. "I haven't heard any complaints from you. How bad can it be?"

"You want statistics? One out of every three

freshwomen are date-raped." She watched the glib look on Jean's face change to immediate surprise.

"You're kidding?"

Moni shook her head.

"Things have changed that much since I dated?"

"Were you listening to "Love Letters in the Sand" on an AM radio in a forty-nine Ford with fuzzy dice hanging from the mirror? Yup, it's changed."

"I'll remember that. 'Old' jokes get added to my secret tally sheet for later paybacks."

"Uh-huh. Well, just plan on staying out of the dating scene. It's only going to get worse."

"Tell me, O knowing one, what do you see?"

Moni stifled a smirk and spread her hands through the air as if opening the curtain on the stage of some future scene. "Keep in mind, "she said seriously. "the biological fact that a penis, once erect, must be satisfied." After a quick glance at Jean's emerging smile, she continued, moving her shoulders and hips to a beat in her head. "You're dancing with your date at a popular night spot — feeling good, enjoying good music. Then some guy squeezes through the crowd and taps you on the shoulder. 'Ah, excuse me,' he says. 'I've been watching you dance from across the room there and, well, it really turned me on — as you can see. And, well, you know what that means. We can use that empty booth over there.'"

Jean was laughing out loud now, but Moni continued. "We all know an earthquake couldn't stop them. Convince a man that it wasn't *him* that made the earth move."

"Okay, okay," Jean said with a laugh. "So we'll go to a movie instead." She disappeared into the kitchen, still chuckling. "Decisions like this make me crave homemade brownies. Want one?"

"Need you ask?"

"Alice B. Toklas they're not, but they do have a certain calming effect . . . Has dating been difficult for you?"

Not if you don't date guys. "Not really." *Maybe this will not go where it seems destined to go.*

"You never talk about it." Then the inevitable. "Anyone special?"

Still undecided, Moni scrambled for an answer. She could let her think it was a man and chicken out once again. Or not tell her it was a teacher. *Shit.* "Sort of."

"*Sort* of? What's his name?"

With a deep, unsure breath, Moni tilted her face to the ceiling. "It's *Katherine.*" She let out a long slow breath and closed her eyes.

Silence emanated from the kitchen where Jean stood motionless, the plates still on the counter. After a few moments of awkward silence, she returned to the living room. "Are you talking about the instructor you've been teaching with?"

"Yes," she said, meeting Jean's eyes directly.

"Has she . . . how involved are you?"

Moni sat quickly beside her. "Jean . . . Katherine is an incredible woman, dedicated and bright. She's been playing a cautious, psychological guessing game with me all semester." She noted the look of relief on Jean's face, but added, "If it was up to me, we'd be sleeping together by now."

Jean dropped her eyes from Moni's. She fussed with her napkin, dabbed at a water drop, avoided Moni's eyes until she couldn't any longer. "Are you really sure about this?"

84

Such loving eyes so disturbed because of her. "About being a lesbian or about Katherine?"

"Your sexuality."

"I've never felt anything else . . . and I've been looking for Katherine since the beginning."

"Then she wouldn't be your first?" Jean asked with concern that couldn't hide her discomfort.

"No, but I won't bore you with the chronology. This isn't how I had always imagined telling you. Actually, I think I always hoped you'd figure it out and ask me."

"You should have told me when you first started feeling like this."

"And what would you have told me, say, at age twelve?" Jean's reticence confirmed exactly why Moni had handled the revelation alone. 'Crushes on women are normal at your age'? 'Don't *worry*'? Wouldn't you have been the one worrying? Just like now?"

Jean's silence spoke more honestly than words. She picked up her cup and started for the kitchen. Suddenly she stopped and turned. "What is she thinking, Moni? She's a teacher."

"Probably that she'll go straight to hell if she falls in love with a student."

Exasperated, Jean whisked out of the room.

"I'm sorry, Jean," Moni called, rising from the couch. She closed the distance to the front door. "I'm going to take off. We'll talk about it another time."

Jean reached the door in time to call to Moni's retreating figure.

"I'll call next time I'm in town," Moni replied without turning around.

With a frustrated flop, Jean dropped among the soft assortment of pillows tossed at the end of the couch. She flung her arms over her head and clutched a pillow to her face. "Ten years your junior, and she knows you better than you know yourself," she muttered into the pillow. *Yes, I would have been just as ignorant as the next teacher.* She stuffed the pillow behind her with a pout. *What an enlightened big sister I am when it counts.* "You have a fool for a friend, Moni," she said aloud.

She gave herself an anxious, unexonerating half hour, then dialed Moni's number. "Will you stop here before you go back to school? I want you to tell me about Katherine."

Loyal as a flag-carrying vet, Moni would be back. *She deserves a better confidante than you, Jean Kesh, but it is you she has chosen.*

FOURTEEN

The end of the semester loomed like a waiting death toll, only a week away. Moni sat on the diving board listening to Katherine introduce the day's lesson. It was the voice she heard in her sleep now, the one she was sure she could listen to for the rest of her life. But once again she faced a future that did not include Katherine. *What am I going to do with this woman? More truthfully, what am I going to do without her?* With a heavy heart she watched the smooth and elegant stride of Katherine Cunningham.

"Moni, will you demonstrate a front dive from the

side for us?" Katherine asked with a wink and a smile.

Katherine held a Styrofoam kickboard only inches from Moni's pelvis. With the effortless ease of a dolphin, Moni cleared the board in perfect form. She did the wet work while Katherine stayed warm and dry. But that's what she was getting paid for. She really didn't mind. Besides, she knew how much Katherine appreciated her abilities. She demonstrated the dive four more times as Katherine explained the mechanics, and then they split the class in half for practice.

A half hour later, Katherine motioned for Moni to bring her class back. They hadn't planned on getting much further today, but the class had progressed very quickly. Yes, Moni agreed, enough time to introduce the back dive. They would at least experience falling backward off the board today. Although mechanically easier, the back dive was the most feared by inter-mediate students. Katherine understood that very well. She was giving them a little dose now, a little dose next time. The transition would be much easier. *Baby steps, Katherine, baby steps.*

Katherine directed Moni to the end of the board and followed. *The partner method. Good,* she thought, *the students can help each other.* It was safe and less frightening — for the students, at least. As for Moni, she would have to endure Katherine's arms around her waist, but only for a couple of seconds. Something she could handle, as long as she didn't look at her.

She took her position, poised on the balls of her feet, as Katherine approached the partner's position in front of her. Then, in a move nearly shattering Moni's composure, she slipped her arm around her waist and held her position through the entire explanation. Falling apart on the inside was one thing, but having it betrayed to the world in a red blush that covered your body was yet another. While her heart beat wildly against her chest and she silently cursed the exciting woman who held her, Moni forced herself to look only at the class. *Do they know the turmoil I'm in? Or, are they too fearful of their turn on the board to notice? Damn you, Katherine Cunningham!*

"Hold the diver with both hands around the waist," Katherine was explaining, while Moni feared the heat from her body must be emitting steam from her wet suit by now. "Wait until their head and arms are in entry position, then let them fall. Their body will follow the path of their head into the water." Katherine stood squarely in front of her, slipped both arms around her waist, and looked into Moni's eyes. "Ready?"

Oh god! Months ago, Katherine. Months ago.

Immediately Moni dropped her head and arms into a backbend, and waited for Katherine to let go. The relief was instant. Water, deeper by the second, engulfed her, cooled her, hid her. She continued to the bottom and pushed off in the direction of the opposite side. She was in no hurry to return to the surface. This was one skill she would *not* demonstrate five times!

For the remainder of the period she worked with her students, while feelings of excitement and embarrassment battled each other. It took concentrated effort not to look at Katherine, not to give acknowledgment to her audacity. Finally it was too much. She looked, only to receive a grin that told it all. All she could do was return a disbelieving shake of her head. *Really, Ms. Cunningham!*

At the period's end Moni grabbed her towel, dismissed her class, and headed for the other side of the pool. A few students remained by the side talking with Katherine. Moni strode up to them, smiled politely, and then nonchalantly gave Katherine a shove. It was totally unexpected. Almost in slow motion, Katherine fell backward into the pool, a look of pure disbelief on her face. Moni continued her casual stroll to the pool office, smiling at the laughter and applause behind her.

"What was that for?" Katherine demanded, entering the office dripping wet.

Moni tossed her a towel. "You know damn well what that was for."

Katherine laughed mischievously while she toweled her hair. "Have dinner with me tonight and I'll apologize," she offered, in the accent that could charm the last sip of Jack Daniel's from an alcoholic.

Will there ever be anything this woman could ask that I can resist? "What time?"

"Meet me at the Hampton at seven?"

"Whoa," Moni responded. "I have made a very expensive point."

"My apology — my treat," Katherine smiled.

"Okay. And I'll have the shower first, too."

"You'd better hurry, or you'll share it."

And anything else your heart desires, Ms. Katherine.

FIFTEEN

The parking lot was filled with status machines: Benzes, Beamers, Jags, Lexuses, and an occasional thirty-thousand-plus domestic for good measure. Katherine's Seville shone respectably under the light between a Lincoln and a Benz. Moni pulled her Escort into one of the few remaining spaces near the end of the lot. She walked the length of the pavement, expecting to awake from her dream at any moment.

But the proof that she was indeed there shone in the faint reflection of the young woman in blue passing before the large, dimly-lit windows. With a skosh more than casual scrutiny, she followed the image in the glass. Could she pass for opulent sophistication, in her one Lord and Taylor dress and her grandmother's necklace? Or was she about to prove herself merely pretentious and young? How long could she keep hidden the little girl with the impossible dream and a thousand fears? And when she couldn't any longer . . . ?

Suddenly there was no more conscious thought, only the sight of an incredible woman in a tight red dress. The very one for whom she would swim the Channel or climb Mount Everest. Katherine turned in the glitter of large gold earrings to send her most beautiful smile, and Moni felt her legs go weak beneath her. "Am I late?"

"Right on time, Ms. Matteson," she replied, chandelier light shimmering in her eyes.

They were shown to a small table near the wall in an elegant dining room, while Moni tried to act as if this were a familiar occurrence. "Our senator eats here, so I guess we're in good company," Katherine said.

"I am in good company."

Katherine smiled her acknowledgment. "I am sorry, Moni, that what I did embarrassed you today. I must admit, though, I'm not sorry I did it."

"Really," Moni returned in her best British accent.

Katherine laughed with genuine amusement and picked up her menu. "What's your pleasure?" she asked. "I'm in the mood for lobster."

Moni looked over the menu from top to bottom — nothing under twenty-two dollars. She was glad she wasn't paying for it. "Stuffed shrimp."

In the course of a delectable dinner and enjoyable

conversation, Moni noticed Katherine's attention wandering toward another table. Katherine smiled curiously and touched Moni's arm. "Check out the couple at the table to your right."

As discreetly as possible, Moni turned in the direction of the other table. At first glance nothing seemed out of the ordinary; an older businessman was having a conversation with a middle-aged woman over dinner.

"Look under the table," Katherine said quietly.

She looked again. Under a folded-up corner of the tablecloth was a clear view of the man's hand as far up the woman's dress as he could reach. She turned back quickly with such a look of disbelief on her face that Katherine burst into laughter.

Katherine shook her head as they laughed and grabbed Moni's arm again. "No, wait" — she managed — "look at *her*." Moni turned in barely controlled laughter. "She's still trying to carry on a conversation!"

That was all it took. They laughed until the tears came to their eyes.

"Oh my god!" exclaimed a woman at the table next to them. And within seconds, the awareness and laughter had spread contagiously to the surrounding tables.

Still, the couple continued in oblivion. Only the approaching waiter, with a dessert menu and a suspicious smile, stopped their X-rated peep show. With an awkward attempt at indifference, they quickly paid their check and left.

"Are we in control here, now?" Moni teased, as she watched Katherine dab her eyes with the corner of her napkin.

"Well I certainly hope so. I'll end up getting us kicked out of this place . . . Then I'll have to apologize, and take you out again. You could get expensive."

"The lobster was wonderful. How was your shrimp?" Katherine asked as they strode across the parking lot.

"A far cry from burger and fries. It was delicious. Apology accepted."

"Are you in a hurry to get back, or would you take a drive with me and talk a while?" she asked, taking Moni's hand.

The move was so natural it didn't even surprise Moni. The flurry of excitement it stirred in her chest, however, would rival winning the lottery. "You make it hard to say no." They continued toward Katherine's car with Moni still a captive of her own disbelief.

Katherine turned the car north and headed farther out of town. "What are you thinking about?" she asked, breaking the silence.

"I don't know. A lot of things." Not really thoughts at all. Only feelings so overwhelming they had no place to go but to dance in her head. She watched the lights of an oncoming car splash moving brilliance over Katherine's face and then leave it abruptly in soft green illumination.

"I assume you know what's going on between us, or you wouldn't be here," Katherine said at last, reaching over and taking Moni's hand once again.

How quickly and easily it was happening, after months of what was clearly a psychological courtship.

"Until now," Moni began, "I was afraid to believe it was possible. Afraid I had missed seeing the line."

Katherine squeezed Moni's hand gently. "I never drew one," she said, turning down the dirt road leading to the county park.

"I wanted to send the right signals without offending you . . . I understand the chance you're taking."

Katherine turned down another road, toward the farthest part of the park. "I've had to become quite good at reading between the lines," she said. "And your signals were marvelous."

She stopped the car, where there was nothing surrounding them except the orchestra of sounds from Mother Nature's most accommodating creatures — and darkness. "Neither of us spoke of a man in our lives, nor a woman for that matter. Is there a woman, Moni?"

Moni met Katherine's eyes with glimmering excitement. "No," she managed, unable to slow the racer's pace of her heart. "Not for a while now."

"Really. Someone so lovely." Her eyes narrowed to a twinkling endearment, her head tilted gently.

And if I'm lovely, what does this woman see when she looks in the mirror? "No one's made my legs weak for a very long time."

"Oh, Moni," she smiled in flattered amusement. "I do that to you, do I? Then I *needed* to hold you up on the diving board."

The laugh they shared was easy and edged away the last of Moni's nervousness. "Why aren't you married to a woman who would rather die than live a minute without your love?"

"Mmm," Katherine cooed, with a questioning brow and love curling the corners of her mouth. "How can you wonder why I'm here with you?"

The look from Katherine's eyes seemed to wrap itself around her heart and hug it hard. In that look, Moni saw herself as something very special, different from being appreciated and desired. She was being loved for something she couldn't even understand — only that to Katherine it was something special.

"What I felt was never strong enough to risk the pain again — until now." Electricity from Katherine's eyes shot currents through Moni's body. "Come here," Katherine whispered, as the touch of her hand spread immediate heat, rushing from the side of Moni's face to every part of her body. With her eyes on Moni's lips, Katherine pulled them together and kissed her gently. Then kissed her again, with almost unbearable tenderness.

"Tell me no, Katherine," Moni whispered. "Say it now."

"I can't," she whispered, opening her lips to meet Moni's with unguarded emotion. She moved her lips freely over Moni's, pressing, then giving in, then pressing again almost fiercely. Moni grasped the back of Katherine's head, pulled her harder into her open mouth, moaned with the intensity of it, and shook from the fierce pounding in her chest.

Katherine closed her arms around Moni, pulling them tightly together. Without mercy for the quivering body in her arms, she explored deeply with her tongue. And Moni held her, tasted her, and gave back every bit as much of herself to Katherine. Her body ached in desperation for Katherine to touch her. And when she thought she could bear no more, Katherine relented, teasing Moni's lips with tenderness, tasting them gently with the tip of her tongue.

Their quest went on, searching with their lips for the need of the other, searching with their eyes for what was in the other's heart. And all the while Moni was falling deep into those eyes, deep into something she had no control over, in clear danger of losing what she had so carefully protected these last couple of years. And it didn't matter.

Katherine's poem seared across her mind, *I'll let you touch my heart, expose it to you whole.* Then Katherine kissed her again, with a passion that longed for expression, cried for release. The intensity was incredible. With a moan, Moni pulled her lips away. "Ohhh, Katherine," she breathed heavily. Her mind wanted this woman, her body needed her.

The wonderful voice was whispering to her, "I want to make love with you."

"Ohhh, yes," Moni gasped, closing her eyes. She felt Katherine's hand on her breast, her teeth gently grasping her earlobe. God, she wanted her. Katherine's lips were laying kisses all the way down the vee in her dress. The top button was already undone.

Suddenly Moni opened her eyes. "Katherine, we have to stop. We can't do this here," she whispered, thinking someone else must be saying the words.

Katherine pressed her forehead to the side of Moni's head. "Yes. Of course. I'm not thinking clearly." They held each other tightly, trying to let the passion subside, neither of them wanting the feelings to stop. Katherine reached for the door. "Come on, maybe if we get out for a few minutes."

* * * * *

Moni took a deep breath and leaned back against the car. She could hear Katherine walking back and forth on the other side. After a few minutes, the steps came closer.

"Legs weak?" Katherine asked quietly.

"Very," replied Moni, knowing that without the car she'd have crumpled into a pile.

"Come spend the weekend with me?"

Something felt like a small explosion in her heart. "Do you think maybe we're moving too fast?" Moni asked, sure that she should say the words, but not knowing why. What she really wanted was Katherine's lips, Katherine's arms, Katherine's love.

"I haven't had an hour free of you since we met. I lie awake, trying to reason some relief back into my life, and it only makes me realize how empty it was before you. I've had to reassess" — Katherine's waving hands came to rest on her hips, and she looked into the black void above them — "everything." She looked at Moni with the gentle smile of a new lover. "I watched you all semester in that wet bathing suit and remembered how good love feels. I didn't think I could feel like that again." Arms now submissively at her side, she tilted her head to the side. "And if that weren't enough — I've fallen in love with you. So there it is, my pathetic story in a nutshell."

Moni looked at her, wondered what it was that she had done so right in her life, and promised herself not to ask why. "And I'm in love with you. And it frightens me."

"There is one thing I've learned to accept, Moni." Katherine spoke softly now, standing in front of her.

"There are no guarantees in life. I'm frightened, too," she admitted, taking Moni in her arms and holding her close. "You can only know what was and what is. No one can know what will be." It was the one thing right now of which she was sure.

SIXTEEN

To the scent of simmering French vanilla, Moni entered the private world of Katherine Cunningham. Furnishings, new and modern, in shades of green and gray, provided the perfect backdrop for surprising dashes of rose and wine, bold statements of contrast not unlike the personality abiding here. She knew, without looking, there was not a hair on the bathroom floor, nor a water drop on the sink.

Moni scanned the room curiously, before stopping at its focal point. Emerging with optical magic from the wall over the fireplace was the partially exposed torso of a bronze nude. A creation of muscle and flesh so real, the eye expected the motion to continue its stretch effortlessly right through solid wall. It was so captivating Moni found herself touching the protruding knee and running her hand along the cool thigh.

"It seems we both have a liking for nude sculpture." Katherine's voice whispered against her ear, her arms slipped neatly around Moni's waist.

"A wonderful marriage of naturalism and surrealism."

Katherine viewed anew her personal piece of history. "The marriage that survived," she offered, pressing the side of her head to Moni's.

"Who's the artist?" she asked, folding her arms over Katherine's.

"Maltie, my first woman lover ... An exceptional effort of symbolism in art, although I may still be considered prejudiced."

"Katherine — coming out."

"You read so very well," she returned with a kiss to Moni's neck.

Her heartbeat quickened, and Moni smiled. "I would recognize that long thigh and beautiful shoulders anywhere."

"Really. I thought she rather flattered me."

"Why don't you ask me in about an hour."

Katherine reached to the little hook behind her neck, and watched Moni step out of her dress in the soft dim light of the bedroom.

"Here, let me," Moni said, draping her dress over a nearby chair. She slid the zipper the length of

Katherine's back, slipped her hands inside the shoulders, and placed tender kisses along the graceful curve of Katherine's neck.

"How long could we have gone on before it came to this?" Katherine asked, closing her eyes at the touch of Moni's lips.

"Not long." Her hands continued downward, peeling the form-fitting dress from Katherine's body. "Not with you dressing like this." Her fingers teased the edges of material covering her breasts, while her lips glided on whispers over Katherine's shoulders.

Katherine turned in to Moni's arms. "Do you have any idea what effect you had in that wet suit all semester?"

"No."

"No?" She tilted her head and grinned coyly. "And always pulling yourself up out of the water right in front of me was innocent?"

"No," she admitted, thinking how wonderful it felt to finally have her arms around Katherine.

Katherine smiled and kissed Moni's face. "No," she whispered, "I didn't think so." Between kisses to Moni's neck, she continued. "You wanted me to see every muscle, every line, didn't you?"

"Yes," Moni whispered into her neck, while smooth, graceful hands caressed and explored her body. Katherine pressed her lips across the broad shoulder, feeling the heat from Moni's flushed skin. Slowly and tentatively, Moni allowed her hands to feel the length of Katherine's back and the curve of her buttocks. "If I'm dreaming," she said softly, "please don't wake me."

"If you are," Katherine whispered, "we're going to dream this together." Her lips teased Moni's, brushing fine strokes over her face and ear and neck. "Mmm, you smell so good."

Moni smiled shyly into the twinkling light of Katherine's eyes.

"What?"

"I have your sweatshirt over my pillow. I go to sleep smelling your perfume every night," Moni admitted. "Did you wonder why I hadn't given —"

Katherine touched her lips to hush her. "It's yours."

"I like the real thing so much better."

"Then that's yours, too," she whispered, her lips touching delicately over Moni's.

Their embrace strengthened. Their kisses exploded with emotion. *And let you claim my body, knowing you'll take my soul.* The words blazed across Moni's mind. The realization of what was happening had almost been overlooked in the crescendo of emotion and heat, the intensity of which was building at an incredible pace. Yet its significance had not eluded her. Moni understood. The risk being taken here was well beyond risking the pain of a failed relationship. And that risk was being taken for her, for her love. Whether worthy of it or not, it was one dream she wanted to dream for the rest of her life.

Heat and moisture radiated from Katherine's back; Moni's hands no longer glided smoothly across it. Katherine quickly released the clasp on Moni's bra, slipping it off her shoulders and letting it drop to the floor. She backed away only long enough to shed her underwear. Then taking Moni's hands, she sat on the edge of the bed and pulled her forward.

Moni stood, intimately exposed before her; trusting Katherine with everything, because she knew she must. She wanted this woman desperately. Her eyes took their freedom of Katherine's body. They followed every line, from the shapely thighs to the dark triangular patch below the tight abdomen and up to the round firm breasts with their dark pink nipples. The vision was even more exquisite than she had imagined. "You're so beautiful," she said softly into the uplifted face.

Katherine's smile was unreserved, almost childlike in its purity. She placed Moni's hands over her breasts and closed her eyes. Tenderly Moni caressed them, feeling the nipples stiffen under her touch. Leaning down, she pressed her lips into the dark, soft hair, while Katherine's arms enclosed her waist. Whispering lips traced the contours of Moni's breasts, sending a shiver through her body.

Moni's next breath raised her breast into the waiting heat of Katherine's mouth. The sensations that followed illuminated her senses to a brilliance that she had not felt since her first time. The warm wetness of Katherine's mouth sent a heated path, flowing with lava, through her body and into a molten pool. Gone was any concern of being desirable enough. Gone was the self-consciousness that had plagued her since childhood. In its place was the desire for Katherine to look at her, to touch her, everywhere. She spread her fingers through the soft hair, closed her eyes, and, with a quiet moan, she pressed against Katherine's attending lips.

"I've tried, Moni," she murmured, nestling between her breasts. "I can't say no to this."

"This can't be wrong."

Gently Katherine slid her hands under the waistband and removed Moni's pants. Then wrapping her arms around her, she pulled her onto the bed. Their naked bodies, flushed with desire, molded softness to exquisite softness, sharing the liquid heat they had created. "I want you, Katherine," Moni whispered, "more than my next breath."

Katherine murmured slowly over the delicate skin between Moni's neck and shoulder, "You are beautiful. . . so beautiful." Katherine's arms held Moni with such gentleness, drawing her into the softness of her body. Her hands lingered over the length of Moni's back, followed the slope of her spine with tickling tenderness, and brought heat instantly to the curves of her buttocks and thigh. She touched her slowly, absorbing the shape of her, the feel of baby-soft skin. Then she withdrew from her to bring her mouth to Moni's, to kiss her slowly, deeply, thoroughly. And her hands continued to caress, torturing Moni with anticipation, stopping for long moments to tease the sensitive places of her breasts and abdomen and inside her thighs.

She felt Moni's body giving in to pleasure, responding to her touch, becoming anxious. She kissed her again and again, tasting her, exciting her, until Moni moved to bring their hips tightly together. The rhythm began between them, slowly and intensely, gathering momentum that soon defined its own perimeters. It sent sensations spreading like wildfire over parched land, searing through Katherine's thighs, sparking kisses that singed Moni's already glowing skin.

"Ohhh, yes . . . yes, I love you," Moni gasped, closing her eyes to center her senses on what she was feeling. "Yes, I need you." She was melting now into fluid fire, losing mind to body, still trying desperately to commit every detail to memory. The feel of Katherine's skin, the smell of perfume in her hair, the look in her eyes, real for the first time. And could be enjoyed as such only once. For never again would there be another first time with Katherine. Regardless of how many times were to come, she wanted always to remember this one.

Memory, though, was on its own. Katherine's hands, delicately cupping and exquisitely stroking, had erased all but one demanding need — to press over and over into their strokes until her body exploded in orgasm. No longer did she savor the slowness, stretching the sensations into tormenting pleasure. The need was too great. Of its own, her body pressed upward, acknowledging every stroke with an urgent, audible breath.

Tension mounted like the swell of an ocean wave, holding her body in suspension. Effortlessly she rode the crest of it, acknowledging its dominion, submitting to it. Her body traveled atop it, going with it wherever it went, enjoying the mystery and the ecstasy of it. Wonderful ecstasy. She rode it, felt it, loved it, until it finally burst forth with a roar, crashing its waves against the shore. She couldn't remember it ever being so powerful or lasting so long. It left her exhausted, filled with an essence and truth so intimate, so honest, that it left not the thinnest thread of doubt that Katherine loved her. And while she gasped breaths of gratitude, Katherine's fingers continued, like quiet gentle little waves, washing the ripples over her until she lapsed into a breathless assent.

With a deep, slow breath, Moni loosened her embrace and held her lips to Katherine's forehead. Katherine's body softened against her in a long, extended sigh. With a whisper she said, "I think I could love you forever."

"I think I'll let you," she replied. "How did you know exactly how to love me?"

"I've always known," Katherine smiled. "I just had to wait so damn long to find you." She tipped her head back.

Eyes of lightest brown held Moni's with an intimacy Moni'd felt with no other. Slowly, lovingly, they stripped away the insulation to look directly at Moni's exposed fear and naked hope.

Moni's fingertips moved with the delicacy of a sigh over Katherine's face. "I love you," she whispered softly.

"I know." Katherine took Moni's hand and touched it to her lips. "And I won't vanish like a vapor now that you've said it. Don't be afraid of your passion, Moni," she whispered warmly over Moni's lips. "I need to feel it."

With the care given a priceless treasure, Moni gathered Katherine to her. The excitement of this body conforming to her own, sliding beneath her, created a new torrent of heat within. Her mouth traveled the path between the sensitive depression below Katherine's ear to the pulsing hollow at the base of her neck and farther to the flesh of her breast, swelling to the fullness of Moni's mouth. Soft whispers encouraged the light circular movements from her tongue. And when she ever so gently teased the roused nipples with her teeth, sharp intakes of breath swelled the breast once again into Moni's enveloping lips. In the midst of a most sensuous moan, Katherine lifted her chest higher and pressed her head back against the pillow.

Whatever else Moni felt for this woman — respect, admiration — it became comparatively out of place next to the fervor of need beneath her now. She tasted the beauty of Katherine with her mouth and her tongue, felt the length of her lines, the silk of her skin. Katherine stroked Moni's back and shoulders while her body responded beneath Moni. Soft murmurs became short gasps of excitement, and Moni no longer doubted that she could please her. She teased the edges of Katherine's excitement with her fingers, and let the words escape hotly into her neck: "Ohhh, what I want to do to you."

"Do it . . . dear god, Moni!" Katherine gasped. "Do it!"

Moni's hand swept swiftly under Katherine's head, raising her mouth to meet her own. She claimed her with intensity, taking her lips, stroking with her tongue as she slid her fingers into the creamy heat. Katherine's gasp only partially escaped. She opened her mouth submissively, took Moni's strokes deeper. Her body arched, her hand grasped Moni's at the bottom of a stroke and slid her in. Taking her with each lift of her hips, each stroke of her tongue, deeper, closer. Until her body, held firmly in Moni's grasp, began to quiver uncontrollably. Sensual sounds, breathless gasps increasing in their fervor, accompanied each slow, deep stroke of Moni's hand, while the pretty hands that had loved Moni so tenderly clutched violently at tangled sheets. Katherine's body, which had moved with her in such fluid synchronization, arched suddenly into a tight shudder. A cry of the most exquisite release lingered long and resplendently in the air. And Moni stayed within, holding Katherine's body in quivering suspension against her while sharp spasms, one after another, gripped her fingers tightly and tensed the flat abdomen against Moni's face. There was no other feeling like it — held within her lover's body, enveloped in her warmth, surrounded in the purity of her need. She would never trade it, Moni decided, even for the thrill of her own orgasm.

Then once again Katherine was grace and silk, easing down onto the bed, Moni flowing with her, on her. Katherine, pulse throbbing from her neck to her abdomen, chest heaving in relief, was to Moni at that moment more beautiful than anything on earth. Moni's lips once more found Katherine's. And as she began to withdraw, Katherine's hand covered hers again. "Stay," she whispered.

"As long as you want me."

Hands of a new artist now committed to memory the shape of an exquisite torso. They moved as if resculpting the gently shaped contours and followed along the sensuously angled lines. Smoothing over its fancy inverted vee and the tight skin sloping to a flat navel, then rising again over slightly protruding hipbones, as if in a final, tactile test of its perfection. Katherine took a deep breath and opened her eyes. "You are truly beautiful," Moni said, looking into them once again. "And this is not a body that needs flattering."

Katherine smiled and drew Moni to her chest. She wrapped her arms around her, snuggling kisses into her hair. "And *you* are prejudiced beyond hope."

"Maybe. But what I fell in love with is what an artist can't see."

"Exactly why I love you," she whispered.

SEVENTEEN

Saturday was a blur, undefined by time, filled only with each other. Edges of lovemaking blended with quiet talk of the past, jumped at times into laughter, began easily again with teasing. At its end they rested, spent as they were, wrapped in each other's arms until the morning light woke them.

Moni woke first, covered Katherine with the sheet, and disappeared into the shower. She tilted her face into the steamy spray. *When was the last time I felt this wonderful? Mmm, never — positively, absolutely never.* She languished dreamily in the soothing heat of the water, wondering how anyone could consider a feeling this incredible as sinful. Then without permission, the thought that anything that seems too good to be true . . . She reached for the shampoo and a symbolic cleansing of the thought.

The lather smelled nostalgically of papaya and belonged linked forever with Katherine. She squeezed shampoo into her palm and applied it generously to the rest of her body. *Do couples living together use the same shampoo? Eat the same foods, watch the same TV shows? Can they tell when the edges of their identities begin to merge?* Knowing you'll take my soul *Is this how it begins . . . the eroding of individual essence, the dilution of what excites one about the other . . . with shampoo?* She would never want to take Katherine's soul or alter it or affect it in any way. She wanted only to admire it, to love it . . . Next time she'd bring her own shampoo.

The shower door opened with an accompanying whisk of cool air. Katherine's hands circled her waist, and her lips drank from the waterfall over her breast, and she couldn't remember what she had been thinking . . .

The gnawing in her stomach reminded her that eating hadn't been a priority since the Hampton. The delicious smell from the kitchen confirmed that Katherine, too, had recognized it. Their futile attempts yesterday had ended in lovemaking on the couch. And later they'd eaten only a few bites of the half-prepared meal, fed to each other between fits of laughter. Moni snapped the borrowed jeans and headed for the kitchen.

"Sit, lover," Katherine directed. "We *are* going to eat, at least once today."

Even the phone, ringing through their first bites, didn't distract Katherine, that is until the caller spoke his message into the machine.

"Katherine, this is David. Don't forget the meeting tomorrow at five-thirty. The room's been changed to the third-floor conference room. See you there. Don't be late."

"Dickhead."

Moni smiled at Katherine's candor. "Isn't that our favorite English prof?"

"He's a favorite all right; the English Department's favorite son. Definitely not one of mine, though. I made the mistake of going out with him a couple of times."

"As in *dated* him?" Her surprise was evident, as well as a sudden sickening in the pit of her stomach. She was not ready to hear that the woman she'd fallen in love with was bisexual. It must have looked as though she was holding her breath.

"Relax, honey. I'm not the least bit interested in men. It seemed, at first, like a harmless enough situation." Moni felt a distinct relief, as Katherine continued. "When I was first hired here at the U, David sort of befriended me, filled me in on department policies, who's who, that sort of thing. We had lunch together a few times, and when the conversation started getting too personal, I became conveniently busy. When he kept asking me out to dinner, I invented a mysterious boyfriend. Eventually, though, with me showing up at too many events alone, he assumed that the door was open. My last line of defense was to tell him I don't date people I work with." She returned Moni's smile. "I insisted that our relationship could only be that of a friend and colleague. He agreed, and I ended up going to the department Christmas party with him. Everything seemed to be fine, but then I really blew it by going out to dinner with him a couple of weeks ago."

"Why? What happened?"

"The evening started out fine. The conversation was comfortable enough — a controversial article in the quarterly, possible assignment shifts for next term, and so on — job related. I paid for my own dinner, and he brought me home. I suppose it was too much to expect that he would be satisfied with 'thanks for the company.' He grabbed me before I could get the door open. When I turned, he backed me against the door and kissed me. I guess I was supposed to be so overwhelmed with passion that I'd beg him to stay and make mad, passionate love to me all night. He's lucky I didn't vomit on his best suit."

"If there's more, I'm not sure I want to hear it."

"Only a small-time wrestling match and a cold blast of the Queen's best blasphemy."

"Why do we have to play that game, Katherine? Let them guess all they want. I won't play it."

"You will have to, Moni, if you're going to teach. Just keeping your home life private isn't always enough. A single woman automatically draws curiosity from other women and interest from men. How will you handle a fellow teacher who wants to date you?"

"I won't let him get close enough to ask."

"Not realistic. You're sitting in the lounge, discussing problems you're having with a student you both have in class. There's a lull in the conversation, and he asks you out. Close enough."

"And I'd politely turn him down."

"And he starts sitting by you in the lounge, talks with you in the hall, visits your classroom between classes. Before long *everyone,* teachers *and* students, know he's interested. And to top it off, he's a great guy."

"I'd have to be diplomatic, or become suspect."

"Exactly. You're playing — whether you want to or not."

"I don't like it. How do you know you're not dancing with a cobra?"

"You don't. It's a guessing game. And each situation is different. It depends on who you're dealing with . . . and I must admit, I'm afraid I've handled this thing with David badly." Worry now showed in the knit of her brow. Her eyes drifted past Moni. "He's not the type to give up easily . . . by his message, you can see he keeps close tabs on me."

"How close?"

Katherine sipped her tea. Her eyes focused somewhere short of the black silk orchids in the middle of the table. Her silence said enough.

"Close enough that I shouldn't be here?"

"Where else would we be? A motel?" The cup hit the saucer with a decisive clink. "Dammit, Moni, this is my home. What kind of life do I have, if I can't even be free here?"

Moni felt suddenly very young — minus some stretch of maturity that should have allowed her to understand that. "I'm sorry. Of course you're right . . . I just worry about causing problems for you."

"And if I were seeing things with my head rather than my heart," Katherine said with a smile, "I'd be worried, too." With a little tilt of her head, she looked with distinct seriousness into Moni's eyes. "Is what we share worth the risk?"

Moni searched Katherine's eyes, looking for some sort of reassurance, some sign that contradicted the fear that it wasn't worth the risk for Katherine. "That's not my decision to make."

Katherine nodded thoughtfully as she came to Moni's side. "It would be nice if I could promise you that we will face no more than the usual difficulties of lesbians in love," she said, stroking slowly through Moni's hair. "Even nicer if I could quell your fears . . . but I can't."

EIGHTEEN

During the following three months, student teaching proved to be all that its reputation had forewarned — weight loss, stress headaches, overfilled days, sleepless nights. Effects that were almost manageable if it weren't for having to take a seminar class, lifeguarding for open swim, and working on the countywide art exhibit. Moni found herself with very little free time, and even less energy.

Yet somehow she and Katherine managed to see each other almost every weekend. Sometimes dinner, sometimes a movie, and always a night of love. Until the last two weekends, that is. Low resistance, and exposure to every virus known to mankind, introduced Moni to her first occupational hazard. She ached and sneezed and coughed her way through seven miserable days and refused to expose Katherine. Then last weekend, although still not up to par, she'd gratefully worked the culmination of the art exhibit. At this point, she would have walked barefoot over hot coals to see Katherine.

Katherine's schedule, already heavily loaded with professional obligations, committee meetings, department meetings, and comp papers, was further hampered by David Shanks. Patience, normally her strength in handling even the most frustrating situations, was proving inadequate. He had become not only an irritation but also a symbol of everything that kept her from what she wanted and needed, a symbol of that part of society that kept her from Moni.

Three weeks, with only infrequent lunches together, were more than either of them could bear. Katherine's choice of the little restaurant forty minutes outside of town indicated to Moni there was deeper concern than phone conversations had shown. She pulled into the parking lot and spotted Katherine's car immediately.

No sooner had she crossed the little lobby than the most incredible looking woman in teal leather pulled her around the corner and into a small hallway. "God, Katherine. You had to wear that outfit," she exclaimed, allowing herself to be pulled into the bathroom.

"You like it, don't you?" she smiled coyly, locking the door behind her.

In an instant, they were in each other's arms, lips

unleashing long-awaited passion, while warm leather as supple as the flesh beneath it welcomed Moni's hands.

"Don't think" — Katherine breathed hotly between kisses — "that I'm only after your body."

"Really," she replied, her lips commanding responses until Katherine was moaning with pleasure. Then she pulled her lips away. Her voice was low and husky. "I can think of *nothing* but your body."

Katherine's smile merged quickly into an impassioned kiss, while imperious hands backed yielding leather against the door. All the time they had missed being with each other was being reclaimed by the fury with which they kissed and the velocity of their bodies' responses. Then in the midst of their oblivion, someone tried the locked door. They separated with a start. Katherine leaned her head back against the door that shielded their secret.

"I can't go this long again, Moni."

"Come on, then," Moni said hastily. "Nothing on their menu is going to feed *this* hunger."

Katherine remained unmoved, looking into Moni's smiling eyes. Her expression was painfully serious. "We've been so careful this far —"

"I know," she conceded with a sigh. "We'll wait until dark." The doorknob jiggled again. "Let's go, before some kid undams Niagara Falls in the hallway."

"What haven't you been telling me?" Moni asked, diverting Katherine's eyes from the menu.

The waitress came and went, and Katherine's reprieve was over. "I don't want to worry you."

"You *are* worrying me . . . *David* worries me."

Katherine nodded. "He's everywhere." The space above her nose was knit into two sharp lines. She looked directly into Moni's eyes. "My classroom, the library, the Union, the coffee house. Always polite, always seemingly with a purpose . . . I'm not imagining it, and I'm trying not to overreact. But even when I changed my whole routine, it was only a couple of days before he began appearing again. He even found your little second-floor library room."

"He's stalking you," Moni said into already troubled eyes. "He is, Katherine. You can't let it go on."

"I've already spoken to Dr. Penley about it, just this week after a department meeting. David wouldn't leave even then, until I said I needed to speak with Carl alone."

"Do you think he'll help?"

"He's my best chance of handling this quietly . . . and the department chair is the proper first step, according to university policy. He did think I'm over-reacting, though, when I explained that I consider David's unwanted attention is a type of harassment." With a condescending pat on Moni's arm, she quoted, " 'You're merely being pursued, dear Katherine. I would guess the poor boy is madly in love with you,' he said with his most scholarly perception."

"*Madly* . . . an appropriate choice of words."

"Mmm," Katherine nodded. "He did promise to have a talk with him, though. But please, Moni, I don't want to talk about him any longer. He already takes up too much of my life. This is our time, and we have so little of it."

They tried to enjoy their dinner, along with a conversation that shared the positives in their lives: their students, the humorously unexpected, the art show. They shared a wonderful bond, and they called upon it now to draw them close and make them laugh. But it was short-lived.

Aware of someone approaching their table, Moni looked up to find a tall man with a close-cropped beard and mustache staring boldly at the two of them.

Startled, Katherine demanded, "What do you think you're doing?"

David Shanks adjusted his glasses and said in a reserved but commanding voice, "I want to talk to you."

"We have nothing more to talk about," she said firmly. "You must stop following me."

He continued as if she hadn't spoken. "When you wouldn't go out with me, I figured you were seeing someone else —"

"Is it that difficult for you to accept that I just don't want to date you?"

"But it *isn't* just that, is it Katherine?" He turned a chilling gaze squarely at Moni.

Katherine quickly interjected, "I don't know what you're talking about, and I'm at the end of my patience." She grabbed her purse and moved to the edge of the booth, with Moni following.

David blocked her exit. "You're a lesbian, aren't you? How can you think *that* can take the place of a real man?"

"Sorry, David, but I have *no* difficulty recognizing the real thing. Unlike you, a *real* man can accept no with dignity." She stood abruptly, forcing him back a step, and spoke quietly but sternly in his face. "Be careful, Mr. Shanks, or I'll be forced to bring charges against you."

"I wouldn't do that," he called to their backs as they started for the door. "You'd be betting your career on academia's tolerance." He followed and stopped at the door. "I'll be having my own talk with Dr. Penley," he shouted into the parking lot.

NINETEEN

She was in over her head, floundering in twelve feet of water with her hands and feet tied. Her body paced the length of her empty apartment, but her mind was drowning. If she stopped moving, maybe time would too. Moni looked at the clock. It glared back its stubborn message: one o'clock. Three o'clock was longer than pacing time away, but she needed to be in motion.

Her roommates returned, and Moni confined her pacing to her bedroom. Every fear she'd ever felt about this relationship was now at its pinnacle. Three o'clock would bring her to Katherine, but probably for the last time. Pacing kept her tears at bay only temporarily, and stopping really wouldn't stop time. She realized there was nothing all her anxiety could do to change it; she must face the very thing she was sure she could not. And she had less than two hours to prepare for it.

If, in fact, Katherine was now seeing things with her head instead of her heart she would end it tonight. She must realize that losing her job and jeopardizing the career she'd worked so hard for would only lead her to resent the very thing for which she had sacrificed it. Her love for Moni would never survive it. To think any differently, to hope against the odds, would be fatally unrealistic.

Every relationship involved a risk of the heart, but Moni had known from the onset that this one involved so much more. Because of *her*, Katherine's career was in jeopardy. All along she'd thought decisions regarding their involvement had to be Katherine's. She was wrong. *How much do I really love this woman? Enough to let her take this kind of risk? Enough to prevent her from taking it?* Without Moni, it was clear, Katherine had a chance to fight David Shanks.

Tears now made their way slowly down Moni's cheeks. She sat catatonically on the edge of her bed, unable to look at the clock. She knew without looking that it was time. Time for her to *be* the woman she had professed to be. And if love was truly what she believed it to be, and she held it for this woman, then now was the time for proving. If for any reason Katherine couldn't say it, couldn't end it, Moni would.

Then she'd move somewhere far away where her soul could die peacefully. The tears kept coming. She didn't try to stop them.

She parked a street away. Katherine didn't have to tell her how dangerous this was. Pulling the hood of her jacket up, she walked along the dark part of the lawn until she couldn't any longer. Quickly she ran across to Katherine's door and, using her key, slipped inside. Katherine was waiting. They held each other for a long time. "I was careful," Moni said, breaking the silence.

Katherine kissed her with tender affection. "I love you," she said, not ready to begin the inevitable discussion.

"I know."

Hand in hand they walked into the unlit living room and settled on the couch. "We have a lot to talk about," Katherine said finally.

Moni tried to take a deep breath. Something wouldn't allow it. All she could manage were short, shallow breaths, and they weren't enough. She felt dizzy.

"Moni, we have to search our hearts and be totally honest with each other. I've thought about this for hours now; there's a lot at stake," she began. "If David does follow through with his threat..."

The tears had already begun again down Moni's cheeks. Katherine tried wiping them away, but they kept coming. Moni stood unsteadily, having made the most difficult decision of her life. "I love you too much to do this to you..." Her chin began to quiver uncontrollably. She tilted her head back to try to stop the tears, but it wasn't possible. The pain of her decision was already unbearable. She tried to continue, but Katherine took her hand and pulled her back down.

"Oh, Moni —"

She forced the words, "There'll be another," wrenching them up from her gut, tearing every sensitive fiber they touched as they spewed from her lips, "less dangerous. Without me you can fight him." She stood decisively, tears streaming down her cheeks. Katherine caught her arm and held it firmly. "Let me go now, Katherine . . . while I still can."

She pulled away, leaving Katherine watching in stunned silence. Moni felt as if she'd been dropped into the middle of someone else's nightmare as she hurried to the front door. Once outside that door she would run, hard and fast, from the nightmare, from the desolation already chilling her soul. And someday, out of the pain, she would come to believe this was right.

Suddenly the doorknob was forced from her grip, the door returned loudly into its frame, and her body pushed tightly against the door by the weight of Katherine's body. Hands on the door, head dropped to Moni's shoulder, Katherine pressed against her in silence.

Moni felt the wet of tears soaking through her shirt and turned in to Katherine's embrace, her own sobs uncontrollable. Katherine's arms tightened around her shaking body and held her. Finally, the sobs quieted into soft gasps that grabbed tiny bites of air with little jerks of her chest. "Shh," Katherine whispered, stroking her head lovingly. Moni lifted her face from the wet curve of Katherine's neck to lips that gently brushed the dampness from her cheeks. "If I asked you to stay?" she said, stopping her lips at Moni's temple.

Her breath caught in her throat, and it seemed her heart did too. Moni struggled to get the words out, to keep from looking into her eyes. "It wouldn't change things . . . you have to let me go."

Katherine cupped Moni's face tenderly in her hand and spoke with a look in her eyes that reached the depths of Moni's soul. "Not just for the weekend."

An almost normal breath stopped short of its goal. Moni tried another while her heart tried to flutter its way out of shock. "What are you saying?"

"That I don't want to teach here — or anywhere — if it means losing you."

The quivering that had begun in her legs now reverberated throughout her body. "Oh god. I don't know what to do," she said, crumpling into Katherine's arms. "I thought this out. I want to do what's right."

"How much do you love me?"

"Enough to give you up to keep from hurting you."

Katherine squeezed her close and nodded against the side of her head. Moni's arms tightened around her waist. "The worst hurt would be the hurt of losing you." She relaxed her embrace and took Moni's face in her hands. "This is a big country. There are other schools."

Moni touched the tip of her nose to Katherine's, then her forehead to her lips. "For so many years I've thought about what love should be like. Yet, I never knew . . . I never imagined anyone loving me this much."

"Nobody knows anything about love, Moni."

Katherine wrapped her arms around Moni's shoulders, cradling her head against her. "Only what we feel when we're in it."

"Can you be so sure that you won't grow to hate me?"

"It's the one thing I can guarantee."

Hope lifted cautiously in the comfort of Katherine's arms. She wanted with all her heart to believe everything was going to be all right. "What about David?"

"We'll figure it out. I promise." She took Moni's hand and led her back into the bedroom, back into her life. She welcomed the arms, young and strong, of the young woman for whom she was willing to sacrifice everything.

Curled together in the solace of the other's arms, they were safe. There were no eyes to penetrate the darkness, no ears to intercept their whispers. And for now, they would forget they ever could.

TWENTY

They faced Saturday with an attempt at normalcy. Time became an impervious vacuum, filling hour by hour with renewed hope and cautious plans. The clock marked time unnoticed while they loved and cooked and laughed. Katherine even agreed to pose, humoring Moni's need to put her on paper. But it quickly became a tantalizing challenge — a game willingly lost — for Moni to concentrate while Katherine removed one piece of clothing after another.

Sunday, however, like the top of an hourglass,

poured time swiftly from its hold. The easiness of Saturday was replaced by a sense of urgency, a need to do all that could be done, say all that could be said, and give each other all the love possible. Even then, what they had left was interrupted by the very presence they'd tried to negate. With total disregard, the answering machine recorded David's message. "Katherine, I can't let you do this. You're the kind of woman that should have a man. I don't know what happened to turn you against men, but you should have given me a chance. Now I have no choice. I can't let you go on destroying young girls' lives."

Just the sound of David's voice made Katherine furious. His message enraged them both. Angrily, Katherine hurled a pillow from the couch against the living room wall. Its muffled impact was hardly the release she needed for the volcano of anger she harbored. She slumped forward on the couch in silence, burying her face in her hands.

Moni stood motionless, hands braced against the back of the couch, and hung her head. It felt as if every once of blood had been suddenly drained from her body. "We've been hoping against hope, haven't we?" she asked weakly.

"We've been trying to hang on to whatever normalcy we have together."

"I'll do whatever you need me to do." She knew she had no other choice.

Katherine leaned back against the back of the couch, reached up, and took Moni's hand. "I need to buy us some time . . . two months. For you to graduate and me to resign."

"Katherine, promise me you'll try everything else

before you resign, please," Moni pleaded. "I can't stand that this is happening to you — because of me."

"Because of love, Moni. Do you think this wouldn't be happening if it were someone else? He's vengeful. He's been scorned. He'll use whatever will get him the most support for his revenge — and give him back some sort of control."

"What? The *moral* issue of love between consenting adults? And they'll support him, won't they?"

"More than likely." Katherine pulled Moni around the couch to sit beside her. "Patriarchy stays strong because of how well they hold each other up. Until now, I didn't realize how frightened men are when they can't be in control."

"They really think they can control love?"

Katherine laid her head back. "Which by its very nature denies all attempts to be bridled, to be contained nicely within predetermined parameters. Allowable here" — she motioned to her left — "but not there" — a motion to the right. "Always wanting to control what they can't understand." She shook her head and grinned sarcastically. "All puffed up with pompous piety, they *control* the *uncontrollable*, while love quietly drifts past their law papers and under their courtroom doors, filling lives with joy they envy" — she held their clasped hands in the air — "and boldly does battle with prejudice and ignorance."

"Who would have thought love would threaten them so?"

"It leaves them helpless. That's what infuriates them." With a sigh she looked into Moni's eyes. "I'll make an appointment with Dr. Penley tomorrow, before he calls me in, and see what I can do."

"You should be writing again, you know — and not just love poems. You have such a talent. You could inspire, educate. Think what you could do with words. You could write under a pen name."

"My sweet, unspoiled idealist." Katherine smiled. "You would have me taking on the world, trying to right all the injustices. But how can I give other women courage or ask them to take risks when I speak from a hypocritical closet?" She stood, with more confidence than she felt. "Honey, I don't even have the slightest idea how to rid myself of one affronted man . . . or what I'll say to Dr. Penley." She turned, with nowhere to go except away from the hope still radiating from Moni's eyes.

"Katherine, isn't there anyone else we can talk to? Someone who could offer some advice or support? Is Dr. Young gay?"

With a sigh, she prepared to erase Moni's hope as gently as she could. "She's gay, and she knows I am. I went out with one of her instructors a couple of times . . . nothing intimate," she assured Moni. "But I know Dr. Young well enough to know she is uncompromising in her demand of professional distance between her instructors and their students."

"But she herself put me in an instructor's position . . . and she's treated me as one."

"You're probably a contradiction she'd rather not analyze. No, this is not a popular battle to support. Rather on the order of supporting your neighborhood child molester."

"I wish you wouldn't talk like that. You're no molester, and I'm certainly no child."

Katherine turned back to face the young woman

she loved so dearly. "No, you are not. But that's not how most people will see it."

Moni reached for Katherine's hand. "What's important is that we know. I've known for years what I want. I've searched for you, prayed for you, waited for you. If either of us has compromised the other here, I was doing the corrupting." She gently caressed Katherine's cheek with the back of her fingers and shook her head. "Don't do this to yourself. I knew what I was doing. I made myself more than obvious, more than available to you. I had no idea if you could ever be tempted, or interested — but with my every waking breath I hoped that you could. All I want is for us to be able to love each other." Katherine's eyes, beautiful and loving, lowered out of Moni's gaze. "There's something besides your career that has you very worried, isn't there?"

She stared somberly into Moni's eyes. "You're far too perceptive for me to pretend otherwise . . . I worry about what this will do to you. While others your age are marching in parades and taking pride in their sexuality, you're sneaking around meeting me after dark. Being with me takes away all your choices."

"What choices are there in education? I'm a lesbian going into a closeted profession. I know that going in. Maybe it will get better, maybe it won't. It's a choice I've made. Neither of us has a choice when it comes to love. I need the kind of love we share . . . I need you." She saw the light brighten in Katherine's eyes. "And I'll take you any way I can get you."

The smile Moni loved so much, the one with its open innocence, radiated from Katherine's face. "For all those reasons someone might say we're wrong, there are so many more that make it right."

Moni took Katherine's hands and backed toward the bedroom. "Then remind me of some of those, will you?"

TWENTY-ONE

"Dr. Penley?" said Katherine, announcing her presence at his office door.

"Ah, Katherine. Come in. Come in. Sit down, please," he said, motioning to a chair in front of his desk.

"Thank you for seeing me on such short notice."

Carl Penley was a balding little man with soft blue eyes and a gentle smile. He was a highly respected scholar and teacher who wielded a powerful amount of influence in the university hierarchy.

"Yes, I had a very disturbing conversation with David last night," he said. "We do need to talk."

"That's why I'm here. The situation has definitely gotten out of hand," she explained. "I've tried very hard to keep my relationship with David at a friendship and colleague level. However, he is obviously having a very difficult time accepting that."

"Katherine, dear, I have to tell you. If I were a younger man, I would certainly do all I could to make our relationship an intimate one." Dr. Penley looked pensively over his glasses. "You are a very beautiful, intelligent woman."

"You flatter me, Dr. Penley," Katherine smiled. "But I trust you would never do anything to hurt me, were our relationship not to work out for some reason."

"Certainly not."

"What worries me is that I think David *is* trying to hurt me."

"You know, Katherine, I've known David for about five years now. He is a brilliant and devoted young man. I sense that he is terribly disappointed that you two didn't work out as a couple. And I can understand, if the things he has told me are true, how devastated he must be."

Katherine knew she had to ask the next question. "What has he told you?"

"He has indicated to me that you've been spending a lot of time with one of the women students, that she has spent weekends at your apartment, and that he has seen you in intimate situations with this woman."

"This is why I'm afraid of him," Katherine

returned. "He has seen nothing of the kind. He is making what he wants out of the situations in order to get back at me for rejecting him."

"What situations do you think he is misrepresenting?"

"The woman student he is talking about taught with me at the pool. She actually has more qualifications and experience in aquatics than I do. We had discussed our lessons and methods over lunch a number of times, and dinner on occasion, depending on our schedules. She is also an artist, and asked me to sit for her. She has worked on a portrait of me on several different weekend days. I will be paying her for it when it's finished." *Not every bit the truth, but not exactly a porky-pie either.* One less lie now somehow made her feel better about the ones to come. Besides, she liked Carl. He had been, unfortunately, put in a bad position.

"Katherine, I want you to know that I am impressed with you as a teacher and a woman. I think I've made that clear on other occasions. And I want to believe everything you've told me is the truth. You must realize, though, that even the appearance of immorality, or impropriety, can be very damaging to your reputation. David, in his present state of mind, may well be thinking that what he is doing is the right thing." Carl leaned back in his chair and continued. "Probably the best thing you can do at this point is to sever all contact with this young woman, and I will have another talk with David."

TWENTY-TWO

Katherine arranged her papers into two piles, graded and ungraded, on the library table. She was able to find a little peace during her lunch periods by working in one of the small library rooms. Her hope that Dr. Penley could persuade David to get on with his life had been overly optimistic. Two weeks later David was still harassing her. Her answering machine had messages from him every day.

His comments to her, every time he caught her alone, had become increasingly crude. Yesterday, he came into her classroom after the students left. "I have everything you need right here," he said, grabbing his crotch. "One time is all it's going to take. You'll be back begging for more." Without a word, she left him standing in the room alone.

She wasn't unaccustomed to having men attracted to her. Their ages varied, so did their marital status. Some possessed more finesse than others, some more imagination. And, like any grouping of people, it included the amusing, the interesting, and the particularly annoying. Yet she was totally unprepared for David Shanks and the loss of ease with which she had always been able to deal with men.

There had even been a time in her life when she had been coaxed into a relationship with a man *because* of his attraction for her. It hadn't taken long, however, for her to realize she could never be happy with him or any other man. She experienced her first woman lover at the university, before coming to the United States. Katherine knew then that it would be a matter of falling in love with the right woman. After a year in the States, she thought she had. Marilyn was a good-looking woman, smart and successful, the owner and operator of a large private camp in Connecticut. After a whirlwind romance, she stole Katherine's heart. Then six years later she broke it. A break that had left Katherine hurt and disillusioned. Her work soon became her therapy. She studied, she wrote, she taught; and she ended up here at the university.

Her life since then could be described as comfortable, and at times even satisfying. When Moni appeared on the scene, a relationship truly was the last thing on Katherine's mind. She certainly had never expected to fall in love with her. Yet Moni

138

Matteson, innately graceful and disturbingly attractive, had an effect that couldn't be ignored. Halfway through the semester, well impressed with her abilities and the depth of her intelligence, she realized she was falling in love with Moni. And no amount of thought or reason seemed capable of stopping it.

The pile of ungraded papers hadn't diminished noticeably when suddenly long hands wrapped themselves painfully around the top of her arms and pinned them to her body. She turned her head into the bearded face of David Shanks and struggled to free her arms, but his grip tightened.

"You've never had a man get deep enough inside you," he whispered hoarsely in her ear.

"Let go of me! Now!"

"The best thing that could happen to you would be for me to lay you on this table and drive into you till I can no longer stand."

He loosened his grip momentarily, and Katherine shook free. She stood abruptly, ramming her chair back into him. Then, sharply turning, she said angrily, "And would that make you feel like more of a man?"

"It would make you feel like a woman," he said, reaching for her.

She dodged his grasp, moved quickly to the other side of the table, scooped up her papers, and ran out the door. She was angry now, much more angry than frightened. Without a second thought she went directly to the president's office.

"Dr. Jenkins will not be in for the rest of the day," his secretary explained.

Determined that her report be timely, Katherine began writing. Before she left the office, she was assured that it would be seen by President Jenkins the first thing in the morning. As a precaution, she also filed a report with the union representative.

Katherine called the next day and the next but was unable to talk with Dr. Jenkins. Finally on the third day the secretary put her through. Yes, he had received her report. No, it wouldn't be necessary for her to come in to discuss it.

"You've explained everything quite clearly," he said. "I'll see what I can do from this end," he replied in a very businesslike manner.

For Katherine, the handwriting was on the wall, in large neon letters. She could expect to hear nothing further from him. She was left to decide whether or not to pursue a grievance, a step that would undoubtedly lead to an investigation her career wouldn't survive.

TWENTY-THREE

Jean's call couldn't have come at a better time. Stopping comfortably short of nosiness, her weekly calls had allowed Moni to bounce the problem with David Shanks off an objective mind. At the same time, Moni knew they were giving Jean a chance to prove her friendship was one both she and Katherine could rely upon. Jean might not have been totally convinced that the relationship was best for Moni, but her loyalty was never in question.

Today, however, Moni needed more than a loyal friend. "I can't stand what this is doing to her ... I'm frightened for her, Jean. He's actually laid hands on her now, and the university has taken no action."

"Do you think you can convince her to pursue the grievance?" Jean asked.

"I've tried. I'm at the end of what I know to do. She . . . *we* need legal advice, and I know she won't trust just anyone. I don't know where to go."

"Remember the in-service I raved about at the beginning of the year? I've gotten to know the woman who did the session on the legal rights of today's woman. She's an attorney here in town. Her practice deals almost exclusively with women's issues. If I could get her over here, do you think you could get Katherine to at least talk with her?"

"You just let me know when and we'll be there, even if I have to sedate and kidnap her. You don't know how much this means to me, Jean."

"I think I'm beginning to. I'll let you know as soon as I have something definite."

Moni hadn't even left the living room when the phone rang again. "Saturday evening, six o'clock. And plan on spending the night," Jean directed. "Ken's up north."

"You're wonderful. How did you get her so soon?"

"I'm not sure. She's either very dedicated or has no social life or both." She laughed. "Anyway, you just get Katherine here."

"I will. But I don't know if I can convince her to stay over."

"I think it's time that I meet this woman. Tell her I'll be thoroughly insulted if she refuses."

"*That* may do it; she's so . . . proper." Moni laughed. Then her tone turned serious once again. "Jean, Katherine has all these acquaintances. She

seems very social and at ease with people. But . . .
they're only professional acquaintances. Not close
friends. Her longtime friends are in England, and so is
her family."

"I know what you're saying, Moni. By the end of
the weekend Katherine will know at least one thing:
she has a friend here if she wants one."

"Thank you. That's exactly what she — *we* — need.
You know, I've never told you this, not in words anyway, but I love you."

"I've always known, Moni. And I hope you know,
although I may not have always shown it, that I love
you."

TWENTY-FOUR

Moni arrived at Jean's alone, a few minutes before six. For reasons she kept to herself, Katherine insisted on driving separately. After a day and a half keeping her hopefulness in check, Moni welcomed the sense of relief Shayna Bradley provided the moment she walked in the door. She was a woman of obviously mixed heritage, dressed in smartly tailored lines, with a presence that filled the room. It was as if Moni's spirit, floundering like a loose chain, had finally locked onto something solid. There was an aura of confidence all about the woman, from the clasp of her handshake to the sureness of her stride. Her gaze was direct, her tone an alluring proficiency. If there was a solution to their problems, Moni quickly decided this was the woman who could find it.

Moni watched Shayna's expression as she spoke and listened intently to the tone of her voice. She overlooked the twinges of intimidation and answered the questions put to her as concisely and un-emotionally as possible. Yet she could not shake the feeling that Shayna Bradley was holding fast to a preconception that held little regard for her answers. Vague get-acquainted questions, a request for a brief synopsis of the situation, with no encouragement to expound. It was pretty obvious. She was waiting for the main attraction — curious to see what kind of woman would find herself in such a predicament, wondering what she saw in Moni Matteson.

"Moni, I have to admit, you're not at all like I had imagined," she said with a cordial smile. "Which is to be taken as a compliment."

"Then I'll try to keep doing whatever it is I'm doing."

"She doesn't have to try very hard," Jean offered. "She came out of the womb like that. I think I've known you that long, haven't I?"

The doorbell rang in the midst of Shayna's infectious laugh, and Jean was finally face-to-face with Katherine Cunningham. In rose-colored pants and jacket, more striking than Moni had been able to describe, Katherine offered her hand.

"Jean, I'm Katherine."

"Yes. I couldn't have missed." Jean dropped her stare from the intriguing eyes. "I'm sorry, come in . . . Let me take that," she said, reaching for the overnight

145

bag. "This is Shayna Bradley, the attorney Moni told you about."

Katherine extended her hand and a smile. "Thank you for meeting with us so quickly."

"It's not a problem," replied Shayna, her face brightening with obvious approval.

"And thank you, Jean, for arranging everything for us." Katherine's eyes strayed as she spoke and fixed on Moni as she moved toward her. "It's very kind of you."

Jean watched as Moni stepped into Katherine's embrace. She continued watching as the smile left Katherine's face, as she whispered something into Moni's ear — watched until Shayna took her arm. "Could we get a cup of coffee" — she motioned — "in the kitchen?"

"We haven't seen each other in almost three weeks," explained Moni, as the two women rejoined them.

"Don't apologize," Shayna said, taking her seat facing them. "If I'm understanding the situation correctly, you have a stalker threatening to expose your relationship." Her eye contact was as direct as her words. "Past the assumption that you are indeed sleeping with Moni, why don't you fill me in on the rest."

Katherine sat stiffly, responding automatically. "David Shanks is a colleague, a well-connected colleague. He's already spoken to our department head and has been sexually harassing me daily. I've made no admission, and he has no proof, but —"

"But unfortunately, we live in one of the forty-one states in America that allows you to be fired on the presumption that you're gay," explained Shayna. "To say nothing of the assumption that you're sleeping with a student."

"You're kidding!" blurted Jean. "Of course, you're not. But I'm surprised that could happen. Wouldn't the union protect her?"

"Unprotected are acts of insubordination, immorality, and incompetence. The three I's."

"But they have to be proven," Jean continued.

With a flair of her hand, Shayna replied, "Insubordination and incompetence. Immorality can be presumed. There is minimal protection in Michigan colleges for their gay staff. But in this case —"

"It's not so much the issue of losing my position," Katherine interjected. "I'm sure I'll be afforded the courtesy of being allowed to resign first, which I plan to do. I'm more concerned with protecting myself, and Moni, from David Shanks. And doing it in such a way as to keep our reputations intact. For the most part, education is not a very tolerant institution, and we would both like to continue teaching."

"First of all, don't resign."

"Thank you," Moni said softly.

"Not yet, anyway," Shayna clarified. "I'll need some leverage. Let me have a chance to take whatever you give me tonight and have a shot at the university. Then if we don't get the results we're looking for, you can file charges."

"And end up in court, fully exposed, *and* lose my job." She maintained direct eye contact with Shayna. "That's precisely what I'm hoping to avoid. Besides, once I lose my job I can't afford to take him to court anyway."

Katherine was hanging on tightly to the thin edges of her patience, and Moni sensed her anguish. She knew Katherine, too, had hoped to hear something concrete, something reassuring. She didn't need to hear what she already knew. Shayna Bradley was going to have to see past the crisp exterior, so uncharacteristic of her lover, and recognize it, too.

"If you're ever in that position because of what I advised you to do, I'll take the case pro bono," she said matter-of-factly. "Look, Katherine, I'd like to talk with you privately. Would you do that?"

"Of course."

Jean stood immediately. "Come on, Moni. We'll go pick up pizza and drinks for everyone."

As she rose something tugged at Moni; a feeling not unlike seaweed wrapping itself around her ankles. In spite of it, she picked up her jacket and circled behind Katherine toward the door. She knew what it was. She was leaving Katherine alone with a strong, attractive, clear-as-day lesbian, with the capability to pull her out of a dangerous situation. The woman she had hoped could offer a solution might also be a clear and present challenge. *Next to Shayna Bradley, how appealing could a yet-to-be-fully-employed young woman, who is a large part of the problem, be?* She hadn't missed how Shayna's professional demeanor had softened in Katherine's presence, or the fact that

148

her eyes hadn't left Katherine's once since she'd sat down.

"Moni, wait a second," Katherine said, producing a twenty from her purse and offering it over her shoulder. Moni took the bill, folded it, then leaned over the back of the couch and slid it neatly down the front of Katherine's blouse. "I'll get this later," she said, placing a kiss on the side of Katherine's head.

Katherine flushed, while Shayna burst into laughter. "You do know how to break the tension," Shayna said. "I knew I liked you."

"Come on, Casanova," laughed Jean. "Let's get out of here before you end up in detention."

"That would be *Cassie* Nova to you," Moni returned. "And I *never* get detention."

"I thought this might be more comfortable," Shayna began, opening her briefcase on the kitchen table. "I need to understand your situation completely . . ." She took out a legal pad and placed the briefcase on the floor. "I'd like you to have confidence in my advice, despite the fact that I'm an attorney." She smiled. "Please feel free to take advantage of me. Tonight I'm free."

Katherine acknowledged her wink with a cautious smile and an awareness of something less than professional. "I do appreciate your taking time for us tonight. I realize your schedule must be busy."

"Not too busy to do a favor for a friend, a priority I won't sacrifice no matter how busy I am." She offered a genuine smile. "And working out every day; another important priority. Strong body — strong mind." She smiled again while her eyes considered Katherine from the table up. "What in your schedule keeps you in such great shape?"

"Are you analyzing me, Ms. Bradley . . . or coming on to me?"

"Beautiful *and* perceptive," Shayna grinned. "Well . . . that depends on how you want to see it."

"I want to see that you've analyzed your prospective client and found her to be uncompromising in her love, willing to give up her job for it if necessary, and in need of protection from a stalker."

Shayna stared, chin resting on her fist, deeply into beautiful but unmoving eyes. "So found. Now, what can I do to help you?"

"Spell out my options."

"First option, file a restraining order, inform the university, and hope for the best. Second, let me go to work on a case against him and file stalking charges. Third, file a restraining order, then file sexual harassment charges against Shanks *and* the university. Or do nothing, take your chances until the end of the semester, and hope that moving puts an end to it."

Katherine took a deep breath and let it out slowly. She leaned her forehead gently on the fingers of her left hand and stared past the edge of the table. "Pros and cons?" she asked finally.

"A restraining order is only as good as your local law enforcement, but it provides a beginning for the legal process. *Sometimes* they work without going further. If we go to court on stalking charges we would probably win, but if he has no prior record he'll most likely get probation. And if he's well enough connected, he may seek revenge."

"Through the university."

"Yes. And even if the allegations *weren't* true, all the media needs to hear are the words *lesbian* and *sex with a student* and it won't matter what happens in court. There is a chance, however, if we beat them to the punch and threaten to file sexual harassment charges, that it may intimidate the university into taking action against Shanks. Then if they refuse, we could follow through with the suit and hope we can keep the media's attention on them."

"What would you guess my chances of teaching at another college would be if it were known that I brought charges against this one?"

"If it were *known*, not good. But neither are your chances that this guy will just quit if you do nothing."

Katherine leaned back in her chair, placed her palms together in front of her lips, and stared into Shayna's eyes.

"Want my opinion?"

Katherine remained stoic, nodding only slightly.

"Let me talk to your union attorney and the university president and explain our position. Put the ball in their court, so to speak."

"And our position would be?"

"If the harassment doesn't stop and they do not fire Shanks, the university would be facing a sexual harassment suit. If they do fire him and he continues to stalk you, we'll be able to go after him personally without affecting your position."

"Doesn't any sort of suit pose the danger of my personal life becoming public knowledge?"

"Yes. But remember you can always drop a suit at any time between initiation and the courtroom steps. A lot of negotiating can happen in between."

"And if he goes to the media?" she asked, already knowing the answer.

"Keep looking for a college where it doesn't matter. Or, change careers." She offered an encouraging smile. "You know, you'd be welcomed with open arms by the gay community if you came out and fought this openly."

"Oh, no. I'm not ready for the chat shows yet. Besides, I have to consider Moni's future as well as my own. Can I think about this during the week and give you a ring?"

"Any time. You should talk it over with Moni."

Katherine nodded. "She's a remarkable young woman, but she *is* young and in love and would do whatever she thought was in *my* best interest." She smiled a rather private smile. "She would have walked away from this, for me, but I stopped her."

Shayna relaxed in her chair. "Katherine, I apologize for my tactic at the beginning of our conversation. Your being a temptingly beautiful woman made it too easy for me to do that. There were other ways of finding out what I needed to know. Maybe not as quickly, but —"

"I know how most gays will see my relationship with Moni. No one will expect it to last. They'll assume I merely satisfied the flattery of an infatuated student — got myself into a mess. And if I can get myself out of it, I'll be on my way."

"It does surprise me that that's not the case. But then Moni surprises me, too." Shayna noticed a hint of pride in Katherine's smile. "No one that age should have such a handle on life. From the moment I walked through the door I felt as if she was scrutinizing everything about me, everything I said, even how I said it, all according to some inner agenda. It made me a little uncomfortable. And I'm rarely uncomfortable."

"That's exactly what she was doing. Beneath that innocent blush and dry humor, there is a depth of understanding that's almost eerie. The kind of raw savvy about human nature that you see in people who have experienced a childhood living through a life-and-death crisis. Their values are in place early. I saw it in friends who grew up in Northern Ireland."

Forty minutes after they left, laughing and laden with bags of munchies and pizza, Jean and Moni burst into the kitchen.

"I don't know," Shayna directed at Katherine. "I think these two have been having way too much fun."

"It's good to see Moni laugh," returned Katherine. "I've missed that lately."

"Has Moni ever told you about her dormitory capers?" asked Jean.

"Huh-uh."

"Tell 'em," Jean urged. "They look like they could use a little levity about now."

"Oh sure," Moni protested. "I had them fooled, and now you want me to blow my own maturity cover."

Shayna snatched the pizza box from Moni's hands. "Okay, no story, no pizza."

"All right, I guess if you've ever lived in a dorm, you'll forgive me," Moni relented. "Personally, I could only stand one year. Everybody always into your business, partying continuously. Guys in and out of the rooms at all hours. It drove me nuts."

"Okay. Scene set. Go on," directed Shayna.

"So, a friend and I decided to get back at some of the worst offenders. We chose one room on the first floor and one on the third floor, waited for the weekend when the place was deserted, and stole the keys from the RA's office. We switched everything that wasn't nailed down between the two rooms, then ditched the keys in the cafeteria garbage." Shayna was already chuckling. "Sunday night we parked ourselves in the main lounge to watch the fun. The first ones back must have thought they were in the middle of a *Twilight Zone* rerun. They tried their key in the door next to theirs, checked the room numbers twice, then started screaming at everyone. But nobody could do anything until the second room was discovered. We laughed so hard we had to leave the lounge so we wouldn't give ourselves away . . . and we never got caught."

They were all laughing now, visualizing the chaos. "Damn, Katherine, maybe you should just turn Moni loose on this David guy," laughed Shayna. "I think she can do more damage than I can."

"Before I accept any *Mission Impossible* assignments, I need pizza."

Hours later Katherine emerged from the master bath, fastening the buttons on the top of her silk pajamas. "Don't bother," Moni said, dropping the shammed pillows on the dresser and reaching for Katherine. "It'll be off before you know it."

With a smile, Katherine squeezed Moni into a tight embrace. "I have missed you terribly," she sighed. "I don't know where to start. There are so many things I want to say and do."

"Start right here," Moni whispered, touching tender lips to her ear and then her neck.

"Jean's sleeping on the other side of this wall." Her warning was given as Moni undid the last of the buttons.

"Or her ear fixed to it. Is that what you're worried about?" she asked, nudging the silk from the beautiful shoulders and trying to control desire that urged like a horse about to bolt for home.

"How quiet can we be?"

"I'd have to be unconscious to actually *sleep* in that bed with you . . ." She felt the response of Katherine's body as she covered her breasts with her hands. "I'll bury my face."

With a sound somewhere between a moan and a sigh, Katherine whispered, "And what am *I* supposed to do?"

"A pillow," Moni said, before her lips gave Katherine no choice.

TWENTY-FIVE

Brunch à la Shayna, at Shayna's, provided something that until now had been totally lacking for Moni and Katherine — social time, enjoyed in the company of people who knew about them and accepted them. And until now, neither had realized how much they needed it.

"Who's going to eat this last piece of apple bread?" Shayna asked, passing the basket to Moni.

"I've already eaten too much."

Katherine broke the piece and placed half on

Jean's plate. "I did, too, but it all tasted so good. What was the cheese dish called?"

"Cheese strata," Shayna answered. "I'm glad you liked it."

"And the lentil-and-walnut salad, and the stuffed mushrooms covered with Gruyère cheese." Jean smiled. "You are a woman of many talents."

Shayna tipped her head forward at the compliment. "I'm your real-life lesbian aberration — a butch who can cook. Karen Williams must be looking for *me*."

"And who is Karen Williams?" asked Katherine.

"A lesbian comic," answered Moni. "A big part of her act is poking fun at the state of butchness."

Jean, although not surprised at Shayna's admission, looked a bit perplexed. "I suspected I might be outnumbered here."

"By lesbians or femmes?" laughed Shayna.

"I don't know . . . I mean —"

"I knew it. My expertise in the kitchen threw you off."

"I've been surrounded by lesbians for years — jock lesbians, to be more precise. I assumed that meant they were butch."

"Ah, physical education — the glass closet."

Jean laughed more comfortably. "Oh, and if I weren't married you'd have *me* in that closet."

"Not as a butch," laughed Katherine. "No matter what closet we were in, you and I would never be mistaken for butches."

"You don't think I'd make a good butch?" she teased, flexing a sweatshirted bicep.

"I'm not sure how convincing you would be" — Katherine smiled — "with a voice like whispering pine."

"Besides, true butches aren't made, they're born," insisted Shayna. "And that's a wonderful description of her voice."

Moni finally rejoined the conversation. "I'll bet Jean's actually more aggressive than most butches. A lot of feminine women are. The terms *butch* and *femme* are back, but the defining lines are a lot more obscure than they were in the fifties and sixties."

"Our resident expert," Shayna said with a grin.

"Ask a lesbian in her sixties what a butch is, then ask someone my age. You'll hear as many differences as similarities."

"I'm not being facetious. You're right."

Katherine looked at Moni. "I've never considered myself particularly aggressive, but I did have to make the first move, didn't I?"

"Then what are you?" Jean asked Moni.

"I'm whatever Katherine needs me to be. That's why it took an eternity for us to get together."

"Ah, true love," quipped Shayna. "Isn't it grand."

Whether or not Shayna held the solution to their problems was a question that had temporarily taken a backseat to the freedom of the weekend. The laughter, and even the mental jousting Moni felt with Shayna, was wonderfully invigorating. Maybe it was an aftermath of Katherine's confirming their love last night, but Moni felt more confident today, more in control. And despite the initial wariness, there was something about Shayna Bradley that felt very right. Even Jean, although she was outnumbered, seemed unusually at ease.

The fact that Shayna Bradley was a woman in a position to help other women, and willing to do so, was to be applauded. There was a certain amount of respect that that alone commanded. And if nothing else, Moni would return to their situation tonight a little less frightened and a little more hopeful.

TWENTY-SIX

"I think you will find the grades on your papers reflect the amount of time and effort spent in their creation," Katherine announced, placing the alphabetized papers along the front of the desk. "Some were a pleasure to read," she said, scanning the waiting faces, stopping here and there at a concerned look. "Others taxed my time. Anyone willing to rewrite their paper will be given the better of the two grades. It will be due two weeks from today. Have a nice weekend, and I'll see you Tuesday."

The students streamed steadily along the front of

the room, each one selecting their paper and then moving briskly to the hall to lift the first page. Grades and comments were always placed discreetly on the second page. They drew the usual quiet mumblings and grateful smiles from some. The others normally reserved their comments for the trip across campus. But not today.

"What is this?" shouted a student, waving his paper and crowding back into the room.

Rather surprised at the outburst, Katherine offered, "If you want to discuss your paper, I'll be happy to set up an appointment with you."

"No, I want to talk about it right now!" Students halted in their tracks as he threw the paper down on the desk. "How many of *these* did you hand out?"

Katherine lifted the page to reveal what she had suspected was a *D* and quietly read her own comments. "Mr. Sims, your composition is full of run-on sentences, dangling participles, spelling errors. You never concluded —"

"I know what's going on here." His comments were directed at the students who had yet to reach the door. "Look at your grades. How many of you *guys* got *D*'s or *E*'s?"

Katherine shook her head amidst their rumblings. "You're way out of line here, Mr. Sims. Your work was graded fairly, as was everyone else's. The fact is, you didn't put forth the effort necessary. If you want a better grade, rewrite it." She pushed the paper back across the desk.

"Yeah! How many girls have to rewrite theirs?"

"Those wishing to better their grade. Now, either set up an appointment, Mr. Sims, or leave my classroom. I have another class coming in."

Angrily slamming his palm on top of his paper, he crumpled it into a partial wad before throwing it to the floor. "Big waste of time without a set of boobs," he sneered. Abruptly he moved toward the door, while those who had remained parted a path.

"I'll expect an apology by Tuesday if you expect to return to class," Katherine declared matter-of-factly.

"Go ahead — hold your breath!" he shouted on his way out the door.

If it had been the only indication, she would have been more able to shake the incident off without major concern. But indications of rumors generated by David Shanks abounded and increased daily. Hushed conversations when she joined the table at committee meetings, overheard comments from students, and stares she hadn't noticed before had convinced her it wasn't her imagination. And if those weren't enough to get the message across, both front tires had been flat when she returned to her car after her last class Thursday.

At first the changes had been subtle, hardly noticeable in a busy day. By the end of last week, however, they had begun to define a very different teaching environment. Gone were friendly greetings from colleagues. Smiles and comfortable conversations were replaced by avoided eyes and politeness, at best. An environment maybe tolerable by some, but not by Katherine. To go from respected, admired, and popular, to shunned and misrepresented was nearly as devastating to her as having found her lover of six years in bed with another woman.

It was all Katherine could do to face the unknown of another day, to look at the sea of faces and wonder which ones had heard the rumors and which ones had not. She looked at student reactions with a different concern now. Was their reaction a response to her teaching or to the rumor? She found herself questioning her natural, and most effective, methods of working with students. Did the young men now perceive themselves as less than valid? Would the women see something more than was intended? She complimented cautiously now, accounted for every smile, watched every word. The essence of her teaching persona had been all but destroyed. Her effectiveness as a teacher was, at least temporarily, vastly diminished. Every day a mélange of emotions taunted her, from frustration to anger to depression. And there seemed to be no relief.

The temptation, the need, to pour everything out to Moni had been kept in check, partially because their primary contact was by phone. Face-to-face and skin-to-skin she would have been unable to keep it from her. Over the phone, though, her command of the spoken word allowed her to spare Moni the needless worry. Instead, after the most recent incident, she called Shayna.

"I realize I'm past the free stage. I'll pay you for a phone consultation whether I heed the advice or not."

Shayna laughed on the other end. "At your disposal."

"Things are happening that I can't directly attribute to David. I'm sure he's started rumors since I'm being treated as if I'm wearing a scarlet L, but I can't prove it. My tires have been flattened and gas siphoned. A student accused me of preferential treatment of women, and today I came home to *Lesbian* spray-painted across the front of my condo."

"Did you make a police report?"

"Yes. It was very humiliating."

"How about what you *can* attribute to Shanks? Anything?"

"The usual daily harassment . . . and phone messages."

"Save the messages. Have you been keeping a daily log as I suggested?"

"Yes."

"Time for a restraining order. How about tomorrow?" Katherine hesitated to answer. "Look, Katherine, whether or not David Shanks actually did the spray-painting or the tires, paid someone to do it, or just provided a catalyst by his rumors, there's no question that a judge will see a connection in light of his direct harassment and grant an order. At least start there . . . and let me sit down with you and map out a strategy. Take it one step at a time if you want." In the ensuing silence, she visualized Katherine, eyes closed, with her forehead resting in her hand.

Finally Katherine said, "I'll give you directions. You can't miss it."

TWENTY-SEVEN

Katherine opened the door, almost stepping on a manila envelope lying at her feet. She tossed it unopened onto the hallway table as Shayna strode up the sidewalk.

"A personal ad would have been much more discreet," she quipped, eyeing the graffiti.

Katherine shook her head. "Pretty awful, isn't it? Maintenance can't get to it for a couple of days."

Pulling a small camera from her pocket, Shayna replied, "Come on down here, unless you want to be in the picture. Grab your jacket first. We may as well get this order filed before you change your mind."

Ninety minutes later, they relaxed in Katherine's living room. As she placed a cup of coffee in front of Shayna and opened the nearly-forgotten envelope, Katherine explained, "I hope you don't think me rude by opening this now, but lately anything out of the ordinary makes me paranoid."

Shayna watched Katherine's expression quickly turn to disgust at the sight of the contents. Shayna held out her hand and Katherine willingly handed over the collection of graphic pornography. Shayna shook her head. "You're not being paranoid. *Paranoia* is an *unfounded* fear." She placed the envelope with her briefcase. "You have good reason to fear this guy. Statistics say that only two percent of stalkers kill their victims, but that tells only part of the story. They don't warn about every manner of physical and mental abuse short of death."

"How did I get myself into this? Maybe Moni's right. I've been dancing with a cobra."

"It's nothing you did. I hear variations of that same guilt from clients every day — something they did or didn't do caused the divorce or the abuse." She shook her head knowingly. "I'm beginning to think I should have a doctorate in psychology to talk to these women."

"All right, doc, I promise to work on the guilt. Now what?"

"You're going to learn to do things differently, but not out of guilt. You're going to do them because you're smart and you want to protect yourself."

"No training in psychotherapy, huh?"

Shayna smiled. "First, unless you're with a group,

it's pants and flat shoes from now on. Second, set up a system so that someone expects to hear from you by a certain time every night."

"Moni rings me every night at ten."

Shayna nodded. "Don't take anything for granted, don't let your guard down — even in familiar surroundings. Always know who's around you. And never put yourself in a position where you could be trapped."

"That's a helluva way to live! He can essentially take away my freedom? Make me live in fear and anger" — she looked intensely into Shayna's eyes — "because I won't sleep with him?"

"Unless you stop him."

"At what sacrifice?" she questioned with a sharp gesture of her hand, then she let it fall heavily to the arm of the couch. "Shouldn't he be getting tired of this by now?"

"Don't count on *that*. There are cases of stalkers continuing for years, many years."

Katherine relaxed heavily against the back of the couch. "He has me cornered . . . like a frightened animal. Never knowing when the cobra will strike."

"And what is the cobra most frightened of?"

Katherine looked appreciatively at Shayna. "Rikki-tikki-tavi." She offered a smile at last. "And you read Kipling, too."

Shayna grinned. "Strike first, Rikki-tikki. Don't wait."

TWENTY-EIGHT

The beam of the Seville's headlights shone brightly across the freshly cleaned entrance of the condo. For the first time in a week it felt good to come home. The visible letters were gone. The ones no one could see, however, remained — in the minds of her colleagues and her students. She had struggled through another day of classes, only to have it prolonged by a glaciated staff meeting and an even less accommodating committee meeting. The best she could say for it was that it put her one day closer to the end of the semester.

As a matter of habit, Katherine surveyed the lighted drive around the car and peered into the shadowed crevices of the building. Tired and anxious for the sanctity of her home, she gathered the pile of folders from the seat. *A light salad, a glass of wine, the soft sounds of Peter White's guitar from Matthew's tape . . . and the sweetness of Moni's voice. At least the rest of the night could be salvaged.*

She hit the door-lock button and pushed the door shut with her hip. Then something to her right caught her eye. She turned in sudden terror at the sight of a dark figure lunging toward her. Papers and folders scattered to the ground. A shout hurled into the night before a gloved hand fought to cover her mouth. His weight shoved her forcefully against the car. The side mirror pushed painfully into her hip as she struggled to free her arm. She tried to scream, tried to think. Fear shrieked against hopelessness. *Is there a weapon? Do I feel anything in his hand? In his belt? No. No. Just keep fighting.*

He reached for the door handle. She nearly fought free before he regained his hold and slammed her like a rag doll once more against the car.

"Please leave your name and number and the time you called. Your call will be returned as soon as possible." It was her brother's voice on Katherine's answering machine. Matthew's idea to deter David, or any man.

"Katherine, it's ten-fifteen. I'm getting worried." Moni hung up and immediately dialed the cellular number. She let it ring. Five times. Six. Katherine was rarely late and was never without the cellular unless she was home. *Did she forget? Is it working?* She looked at the clock again and reminded herself not to panic. *How late is too late?*

"Open the door!" he growled.

His arm, wrapped tightly around her chest and arms, allowed only the use of her right hand. He pulled Katherine back just enough so that she could reach the keyless entry. *Maybe he only wants the car.* She said it as clearly as possible into his hand. "You can have the car."

"Open it, cock-teaser," he demanded. "And get in."

No! Oh, no. I cannot get in the car.

"Now!"

She raised her hand to the keypad, and tried again to talk into his hand. "I can't see it."

The tension eased on the hand covering her mouth. Katherine lowered her head as far as he allowed; then with all the force possible she threw her head straight back into his face. Her aim was perfect, slamming against his nose.

With an exasperated groan, his grip softened, and in an instant she was free. Her steps, staggered and shaky with adrenaline, drove her momentarily from his reach. He lunged. She twisted away from the car and began to run. Her strides lengthened, stretching for the street. Her own breathing covered the sounds of her feet against the pavement. His labored grunts sounded close behind. A face appeared in a window on a lighted porch. Step after running step, she strove not to be grabbed from behind. She shouted out for help. The face disappeared behind the curtain. The porch went dark.

"Two cars have been dispatched to that location," said the officer on the other end. "If you have information that could be helpful, please talk with the officers at the scene."

In that moment her heart ceased to beat and her chest tightened around its last breath. The phone dropped from Moni's hand. Eyes stared blankly from their nightmare, then darted from their paralysis in a frantic search. *Keys, keys! Think, dammit!*

They were there, thrown casually to the center of the kitchen table and grabbed now in haste. Down the stairs she hurried, stumbled, numb with fear, trying to discourage her worse thoughts. *Not Katherine. Please not Katherine.*

Three times she started the car. Three times it stalled. Finally, with one foot on the accelerator and the other on the brake, she narrowly missed the truck behind her and surged from the driveway. She raced without thought through stop signs and gas stations, cursing aloud and praying in silence.

Katherine reached the porch from the sidewalk in one leap and pounded her fist against the door. "Please! I need help!" She dared a look behind her. The sidewalk was deserted. She pounded again. "Please! I'm alone. I need help." She was afraid to leave the porch to try another house. *Please answer the door!* She knocked again, then surveyed the darkness beyond the porch.

Suddenly the door opened and a man pulled her inside. Breathlessly she gasped, "Thank you. Thank you. Please ring the police."

"My wife called," he said, directing her to the couch. "Are you hurt? Do you need an ambulance?"

All at once she felt as though the puppeteer had dropped the strings that held her, and her body collapsed limply onto the couch. She took a deep, still shaky breath, and shook her head. "I'm all right." Weakly her trembling hands tried to gather the gaping material of her blouse, stripped of its buttons, and tuck the ends into her waistband.

A heavy woman with blue-gray hair appeared next to her with a cup of coffee and a comforting arm round her shoulders. "Is there anything I can get you?" Katherine shook her head. "Did he hurt you?"

"I'm just bruised . . . and frightened."

"Of course you are," she replied with noticeable concern.

"Was this a husband or boyfriend?" the man asked, peering out the darkened window from the edge of the curtain.

"No . . . I don't know who it was. He had on a ski mask."

"We heard you yell. I'm sorry. John thought he may have had a gun."

Katherine nodded. *If he had, I would have been dead, and no one would have helped.* The thought made her shudder.

"The police are here," he said, starting for the door.

Armed with the description Katherine knew was hopelessly insufficient, the police began their search.

Moni stopped behind the empty squad car and bolted from her seat. Without a second to close the door, she ran to Katherine's drive. It was littered with books and papers and Katherine's purse. The beam of a large flashlight preceded an officer around the corner of the building.

"Katherine Cunningham" — she panted — "is she all right?"

He walked closer before answering, shone the flashlight behind her. "Seems to be, but she's pretty shook up."

Thank you. Thank you. Thank you. "What happened? Can I see her?"

"Wait across the street there." He pointed to the lighted porch and offered nothing more.

Moni paced for minutes, back and forth across the porch, thankful, anguished, angry. She settled on the steps, while the realization of what could have been burst forth in a torrent of tears. She buried her face in her hands, until finally the worry and fear dissolved with her tears into relief. Then only the questions remained. As desperately as she wanted answers, they would mean nothing without Katherine's safety. Nothing was worth jeopardizing that, not a job, not even justice. If Katherine wanted to resign, she would not argue with her. And she would not be leaving her alone again. In fact, they were getting out of there tonight.

The door opened behind her. Without reservation Katherine stepped into Moni's embrace. "It's okay," she said, as if Moni were the victim. "I'm okay." In her eyes, though, was a solicitude that was going to take more than the embrace of a lover to erase.

"We're going to check the grounds once more, then make sure your house is clear," the officer coming up the steps informed them. "It would be a good idea to go to a friend's tonight, or have someone stay with you."

"I'm staying," Moni replied.

In the darkness of their privacy, Katherine held Moni tightly. Tears didn't come often or easily, but they came now, flowing quietly and unnoticed by Moni until their warmth touched the skin of her neck.

Moni stroked the soft dark hair. "Everything's going to be all right, honey. You know I love you." She felt a gentle nod against her ear. "Do something for me." Katherine straightened and wiped the wetness from her cheeks. "Pack a suitcase, a big one."

TWENTY-NINE

"It wasn't David," Katherine said, staring out the side window. Moni took her eyes off the road long enough to look at her.

"Are you sure?"

"He was no taller than I am," Katherine returned. "I must have broken his nose."

Moni reached over carefully. "How's your head?"

"A little tender, but not nearly as painful as what this is doing to me emotionally."

"That's another reason why we have to get out of here."

"*That* bothers me, too. I feel like I'm running scared, like I'm losing my self-dependency."

"You are scared, and so am I. We'd be foolish not to be. You'd be the first to tell *me* that, if the situation were reversed . . . wouldn't you?"

"Yes, I would," Katherine relented, leaning back in the seat with a sigh. "How'd you get so smart?"

Moni looked over at Katherine. She looked so tired, her face pale and drawn. She wished she could hold her. "You're exhausted. Why don't you lay the seat back and try to sleep. It'll be three o'clock before we get there."

"I should talk to you . . . keep you awake."

"I'll be fine. If I start getting tired, I'll wake you up, okay?"

"Okay," she said, her voice just above a whisper. "You could talk me into anything, Moni Matteson."

Jean answered the door of Shayna's house, and hugged them each warmly.

"Thank you, Shayna," Moni said. "My parents would not be able to handle this yet."

"I had to tell Ken, Moni," explained Jean.

"I was afraid of that. Has he disowned me?"

"We'll talk about it later."

They were barely seated on the couch when Shayna began her barrage of questions. "I'm sorry this happened, Katherine. You're sure you're all right?"

"Just bruised."

"And you said it wasn't David Shanks? Are you sure of that?"

"I'm sure. He was shorter and heavier."

"How did it happen?"

"He came out of nowhere. I checked carefully before I got out of the car. He must have hidden around the pine tree."

"Then I don't think this was random. He was waiting specifically for you."

"The police said the same thing. They interviewed the neighbors, and no one saw him hanging around earlier."

"He knew your schedule."

"Maybe. I have to provide a list of everyone who knew I had meetings last night, although I doubt it'll do much good."

"It includes Shanks."

"You think he's responsible, too, don't you?" Moni asked.

"It's possible. Did this guy say anything?"

Katherine shrugged. "Not much. 'Open the door,' 'Get in.'" Her eyes darted sharply back to Shayna's. "He called me a cock-teaser."

Shayna nodded. "That possibility just became a probability."

Jean finally joined the conversation. "You think he went to that extent to scare her?"

"Or worse." Shayna leaned forward in her chair. "What would have happened if that guy had gotten you in the car?"

"What are you saying?" Katherine asked.

"How difficult do you think it would be to hire someone to rape you?"

"I don't want to believe David's capable of that. He is an egotistical man who doesn't bear rejection well. But he is also a gifted, passionate teacher. This attack could be merely a repercussion of the rumors."

Shayna looked at Jean and shook her head in frustration. "It's too bad for Mr. Shanks that it's past the point of what *you* want to believe."

"How realistic is it to expect the police to find a connection to Shanks, or even to find the attacker?' Moni asked.

"Statistics aren't in our favor. But personally, dead ends have always looked to me like perfect places for someone to get trapped."

Moni smiled. Shayna's coy confidence sent a charge of bravado through her. "What can I do to help?"

"Find out what the students think about the passionate professor." She noticed the disconnected stare in Katherine's eyes. "I'm not making decisions for you, Katherine. I understand your dilemma. You don't have to pursue anything. You make up your own mind about that. But realize that with the police involved now, some of this is out of your control."

"Well, I do still have a shred of control left. I've been watching the job bulletins. There are a couple of things out there, and I'm sending my résumé. If I get an interesting bite before you do, I'm going to take it."

"This is getting dangerous, though, Katherine," advised Jean. "Please let Shayna help."

"She doesn't have to *let* me do anything. This is a personal thing now." Her eyes, direct and certain, came back to Katherine's. "There's one thing you should know about me. Once I sink my teeth into the skull of a cobra, I hang on till it's over."

THIRTY

Heat rose in Dali-like waves above the rows of asphalt-black robes seated in the middle of the football field. Sweat beads tickled a path down Moni's sides, while humid air laid so still it resisted normal efforts to move it in and out of her lungs. Granted, no one had predicted record-high temperatures for graduation day, but an outside ceremony in ever-changing Michigan weather still seemed an irrational decision.

She searched the honored faculty who were seated on either side of the podium and dressed in varied colored stoles. She found Katherine first and then quickly reassured herself that David Shanks was nowhere close, finding him at the opposite end of the row. Decisions made by highly educated persons didn't guarantee that they were based on sound judgment or fairness. And the university was proving to be a prime example of this. It now came as no surprise to Moni that decisions were often based on personal agendas and private prejudices. Maybe they really believed the world of academia was a proving ground for the world at large. Maybe they were unaware of corporate America's shift toward respecting diversity, even if it did so only to avoid costly legal battles. Or maybe they were just arrogant enough to ignore it.

Whichever the case, the university was still protecting David Shanks, not because he made Shakespearean characters as familiar to his students as Tom Cruise, but because he was a heterosexual white male. Katherine Cunningham, as talented as she might be, would not be afforded the same consideration. For all its advances over the past half century, the women's movement could claim no inroads into academic conscience here. Unless it was forced legally to do otherwise, the university would continue to follow the policies of its patriarchal ancestors. Dinosaurs breathing ancient dust. How far off could extinction be?

She had done as Shayna had asked. In a period of five days she had found out more about David Shanks than she cared to know. Male students, if given the chance, would put him in the White House. Female reactions varied. Some were able to separate the professor's personal egotism from his classroom effectiveness; some didn't see it at all. And the one whose hand just might be covering the can of worms Shayna swore was there was nowhere to be found.

Yet Shayna kept looking with a determination that could be defined as either admirable or suspect. What made this a personal case for her, was what Moni wanted to know. *The injustice, the helplessness? Or an attraction to Katherine?*

"Your professors have prepared you to go forth from here, ready to take this country into the next century," the senator was saying. "Among the tools they have given you to accomplish that task is a disciplined mind . . ."

Irrelevant.

"Knowledge . . ."

Of a slanted playing field.

"Skills, specific to your role in an ever-changing world . . ."

But not to a game with ambiguous rules and biased officials. Who was he talking to? The Hispanic woman sitting in front of her? The black woman two chairs away? The man in the wheelchair at the end of the third row? Moni Matteson? All prepared to win and looking for a team that would take them. And the only one among them with half a chance was a lesbian, the only one able to lie to the world for that chance.

She looked down her row to see if anyone was actually listening. The sight made her smile. Most robes were unzipped and opened. Exposed beneath them were bright-colored beach shirts, halter tops, and even the bare chest of an imprudent male athlete. *What a view the senator must have. Amazing how he continues without a glitch.*

The row in front of her was nearly finished receiving their diplomas. Moni zipped her robe over a conservative sleeveless blouse and stood with her row. With a sense of anxious relief she awaited her name.

"Monica Kay Matteson."

At last. She walked tall up onto the platform, graciously accepted her diploma and the hands shaking hers in congratulations. Straight ahead she found Matthew and smiled for the proverbial family-album picture. The pride his smile sent back to her made her glad he was there, along with her parents and Jean and Ken. Initially, this had meant more to them than to her. Yet despite the ceremony itself seeming a ridiculous waste of time, Moni had to admit she felt wonderful right now.

As discreetly as she could, she found Katherine's eyes before leaving the platform. The envelope on her lap was her resignation; the smile on her face was reassurance. Moni ceremoniously crossed the tassel over and stepped down. *For all the sacrifice Katherine is making, is it possible that now we are free?*

THIRTY-ONE

"I think I may have a break." Shayna's cut-to-the-chase manner was familiar now. Phone conversations began as if they were face-to-face.

"Have you told Katherine?" Jean asked.

"Left a message on her machine. I may have found Lisa Becker. I've been leaving messages all over this town. I finally got a call back. If the rumor is true, she could do some real damage to Mr. Shanks."

"After all this I hope she's the right woman."

"*I* hope she's not afraid of snakes. If Katherine calls, tell her I'll call her tonight."

* * * * *

It had been a frustrating week of wrong addresses, old phone numbers, and collecting information from reluctant old boyfriends and family members. Shayna had spent many unpaid hours and uncounted phone calls, but three cities later she was about to find out if it was all worth it. She knocked on the apartment door.

"Lisa Becker? I'm Shayna Bradley. As I explained on the phone, I'm investigating David Shanks for possible sexual harassment charges."

Lisa Becker was every bit what she expected, a sorority woman with looks and social graces capable of doing as much, or more, for her future as good grades. "I don't know how much help I can be, but I'm curious about what's going on."

Shayna's brief synopsis did not include the fact that her client wasn't really a client, or that being a lesbian had stopped her cold in her tracks. She needed to put Lisa Becker in a comfort zone. And there was always comfort in thinking you're not alone. "Your name came up in the course of my investigation. Did your leaving the university two years ago have anything to do with David Shanks?"

"It had everything to do with him." She hesitated long enough to take a full drag from a freshly lighted cigarette. "I was majoring in English lit and took a required course from him in my junior year. Have you ever done something that you knew at the time was a bad decision, but you did it anyway?"

"Haven't we all?"

Lisa smiled quickly and swept her fingers through

shoulder-length brown hair. "I'd dated a lot of guys without any real problems, but I guess I was still naive." Shayna waited patiently while Lisa struggled with baring her soul to a stranger. "When you know someone like him is interested in you . . . well, it's flattering. Anyway, I slept with him."

"So when did the problems start?"

"When I decided not to do it again. He's not good in bed; he's rough and domineering. I was going to chalk it up to experience and forget it. Then he started threatening me."

Bingo! "How?" *Go on, honey, knock the lid off the can.*

"I really didn't take him seriously at first. He kept calling, and I just blew it off. Then, when my papers started coming back with failing grades, I knew he was serious." She shook her head slowly. "I gave in to him to pass the class, and then I quit school. He was the only one teaching a major class I needed to graduate the following semester, so I transferred and graduated last year."

"Did you ever make a complaint?"

Lisa nodded, took a long drag from her cigarette. "He turned it around, told the dean right in front of me that I'd been coming on to him. He said I was the kind of young woman who, if she could, would sleep her way through all the tough courses."

"And they believed him. Have you ever thought about bringing charges against him?"

"No. I figured since he didn't rape me, there was nothing I could do. I just wanted to graduate and get on with my life."

"Sexual harassment *is* a type of rape. It's also a

violation of Title VII of the Civil Rights Amendment. The law's on your side. You have every right to take this man to court."

"What about your client? If you win that case, he'll do some time for that, won't he?"

"Maybe, maybe not. It's not as strong a case as yours. The punishment, if there is any, could be lenient. Besides, I don't expect her to follow through with the suit. You are my best chance to get to this guy."

"I'm a first-year teacher, untenured. Last year I'd have done it in a minute. Now I'd have to worry about administrators, parents, and even students finding out what it was all about. Plus, I'm still paying off loans. I don't have the money."

"Men like David Shanks have been allowed to hide behind the respectability of careers and social status far too long. It's time women send them a message. Since I'm in a position to help do that, I'm willing to take the case pro bono." Shayna took a card from her case and offered it as she stood.

"Don't get me wrong. I despise this man. He humiliated me . . . he made me feel like a whore. What I did for a grade was disgusting." She looked Shayna directly in the eye. "For that semester I became what he told the dean I was."

"Then go after him. Do you want him to keep doing this to other women?"

"No. But I won't give him a chance to dirty anything else in my life."

"I don't want you to do anything that would harm your career, but do one thing for me. Talk with administrators and teachers and anyone else you trust, before making up your mind."

"I promise I'll think about it, but I doubt I will change my mind."

"He'll continue until someone stops him, Lisa. All I'm asking is for you to think it through thoroughly."

THIRTY-TWO

"We should be taking *you* to dinner for helping us move," Katherine declared, seating herself at Shayna's dining table. "Being able to relax again in a room that's not piled full of boxes feels wonderful. The excitement of moving loses its appeal in a hurry when you can't find your underwear."

"Only a temporary state of confusion." Shayna smiled. "A month from now you'll be looking for something permanent."

"Have you heard anything from any of your interviews?" Jean asked.

She nodded. "A couple."

"She's being modest," explained Moni. "She's been offered a position at Braxton. They had the second highest academic ranking for community colleges in the country last year."

"That's wonderful!" exclaimed Jean. "You're going to take it, aren't you?"

"If Moni gets something within driving distance. I don't want to rush the decision."

"Don't wait for me, honey. The president's going to offer his first-born male child if you don't accept soon." She squeezed Katherine's hand before seating herself across the table. "I can sub until something comes up."

Shayna reappeared with a bottle of wine. "Katherine, did you have time to finish those papers I gave you?"

"Right here," she said, retrieving the folder from the table in the corner. "And my curiosity is off the chart. I recognized the assignments as David's. The papers all seem to be the work of one person."

Shayna filled each wineglass and raised hers to signal a toast. "To good friends, new beginnings" — her eyes met Katherine's as the four glasses touched over the table — "and the courage of Lisa Becker."

"She's going to do it!" Katherine sprang from her seat and grabbed Shayna in an enthusiastic embrace while Jean and Moni watched. "I had given up on her."

"Ah, ye of little faith," smiled Shayna. "I suspected the more people she talked to about it, the more angry she'd get. And I was right."

"Lisa Becker," Jean mused. "Who'd have thought. First-year teachers are frightened of their own shadow.

Until you're tenured, you never do anything controversial. You never support strikes or withhold services. And you're *very* careful who on staff you befriend. They don't have to tell you why you're not asked back."

Katherine nodded. "She must have been very angry."

"So were those her papers Katherine evaluated?" asked Moni.

"Yes, from David's class as you suspected." She directed her attention to Katherine. "How'd she do?"

"There was only one I would have given a *B*-minus; the rest were *B*-plus or better."

"Take a look at these."

Katherine skimmed through page after page. "Over-generalized comments, lines through sentences with no comments, demeaning criticisms."

"And tell me how a student can go from *A*'s on the first two papers to *E*'s on the next three, and back to *A*'s on the last two?"

"Anyone would be immediately suspicious. Didn't she go to the dean?"

"After Professor Shank's character assassination, he wouldn't take her complaints seriously. She gave up and gave in."

"I'm embarrassed that this could happen in education," Jean interjected. "I guess we've come to expect it in the corporate world — but education?"

"Are the papers going to be enough proof?" Moni asked.

"Not by themselves. But arrogance begets stupidity. He checked them into a motel using his own name. Plus, a sorority sister is willing to testify to an argument she overheard between them in his office.

"This is nothing new to you. You were willing enough the first time" doesn't sound like a critique of Shakespeare."

"Did I get you the right lady?" boasted Jean. "My money's on her taking this to the end and winning."

With a tilt of her head, Katherine smiled. "You do indeed sink your teeth in."

"I only regret I couldn't have gotten this far before you made your decision to resign."

"The university has been a good place for me. But the damage has been done. It's time to move on. It is nice to know, though, that you may be able stop David from ruining someone else's experience there."

"Haven't I lifted your faith, yet?" Shayna smiled. "We *will* stop him."

Moni listened with a distracted ear to Jean's exposition of Shayna's efforts over the past weeks. Meanwhile, Katherine remained in the kitchen with Shayna. The dishes were done, the food put away. She could think of no conversation that couldn't, or shouldn't, be shared. *Had it been ten minutes? Fifteen? How long a time would be considered rude . . . or worse?* She took a deep breath and tried to concentrate on what Jean was saying.

". . . more women like her to help empower women, to lift them up until they can stand on their own. I've never seen such a unique combination."

True, Moni conceded. She wanted to like her, too. It wasn't really that she didn't like Shayna *or* respect her. But Moni's champion, if she was to have one, had to be totally trusted, beyond the doubt of selfish intent or personal gain. Besides, there had been no miracles pulled off here. Katherine had resigned. They had moved on their own volition, plotting a future based on their own merits. Any other attorney, paid or not, would have considered it over. All Moni wanted to know was why Shayna had not. Shayna Bradley didn't have to be a saint, she decided, as long as she wasn't a sinner.

"Jean, we were considering extending our celebration and making a night of it," Shayna said, almost too politely. "These two have never been able to really go out. They've never even danced together."

"But we want you to be part of our celebration," Katherine added. "So we won't go anyplace where you would feel uncomfortable."

Moni monitored Jean's expression. She sensed a reaction similar to her own on many occasions — wanting to be included but not wanting to be embarrassed.

"I guess I wouldn't worry about students. Mine are too young for the bars. But . . ."

"There's a club about an hour from here," Shayna explained. "Far enough away, with an older, more professional crowd. It's as close to being safe as we have."

"Would Ken be okay with this?" asked Moni.

"He's at the hockey game. He won't be home until late . . ." She looked at Moni and shrugged. "I'll leave him a message. Let's go."

THIRTY-THREE

"Ever been in such a decadent place, Ms. Kesh?" laughed Shayna.

"Does the teacher's lounge count?"

"Oh god, yes!" exclaimed Katherine, as they laughed.

Moni lifted her glass and the others met it. "If it's a place filled with smoke and gossip, and varying degrees of hiding your real self from the masses, I'll be able to relate."

"Were you a bar girl, Moni Matteson?" Katherine grinned.

"Disgusting, isn't it?" she said, reaching for Katherine's hand. "Come on, dance with me."

In her arms, publicly for the first time, Katherine followed Moni's lead effortlessly. Pride wasted no time in its claim, as more than one woman gave them notice. A beautiful, intelligent lover in her arms, and a place, however disorganized and tentative, where they could finally be together. Happiness should be at its pinnacle. *So what weighs so heavily on the wings of my excitement? Fear of David Shanks, who may have sealed his own fate? A private talk with Shayna in the kitchen for fifteen minutes? Or a more subtle fear that when all clear and present threats are abolished there will remain only my own inadequacy? And which do I fear most?*

"I love the way you move." Words, on a whisper that stilled her fears. Moni kissed the tender skin in front of Katherine's ear. "Maybe we should make our excuses, and go make love among the boxes."

Moni smiled against the soft cheek. "Maybe you shouldn't suggest something you have no intention of doing."

Laughter rang from their table. "The look on Ken's face was priceless," Jean finally managed. "He'd totally forgotten Moni was going to be there."

"Willie Wanna and I have a stand-up idea," Moni teased, sending them into laughter once again. " 'Come on in here and lie down, and we'll discuss it' . . . just in case at sixteen I didn't have a clear enough vision of what *afternoon delight* was all about."

Jean wiped tears from her eyes. "I don't know who was most embarrassed. He spent the rest of the day trying to make up for it."

"I don't think he stopped talking for four hours." Moni's smile suddenly dissolved into a pensive frown. "He hasn't been very talkative lately."

"Give him time, Moni."

Shayna rose and draped her blazer over the back of the chair. "This sounds a little personal," she said, leaning over Katherine's shoulder. "Let's dance."

Maybe Moni wouldn't have been so distracted or her chest so constricted just trying to take a normal breath if the music that was bringing the women to their feet hadn't been so slow. The thought of Katherine in Shayna's arms blocked all but the notes from her consciousness. Jean's lips were moving, but the words weren't registering. She tried to force the vision from her mind as Katherine's figure disappeared into the slow-moving crowd.

"You've always been like a younger sister to us," Jean's voice became clear again. "In fact, I think Ken imagines you as what he would want a daughter to be like. Someone who shares his interest in making things, who he can teach things to. Someone who actually enjoys fishing with him."

"Maybe he doesn't feel that way anymore."

"He'll be fine, Moni. He just needs some help getting over the hump. You need to show him that you haven't changed. Come and spend a day with him."

"If you think it would help."

"All right, who's going to dance this one with me? I'm not ready to sit down yet," Shayna grinned.

With both Jean and Katherine pointing at her, Moni had no reasonable way of refusing. *At least Shayna won't be dancing with Katherine.* "We'll bring fresh drinks on our way back," she said, turning toward the dance floor.

"Everything okay?" Katherine asked.

"It's hard to watch people you love in so much emotional pain." Katherine rested her chin in the palm of her hand, and gave Jean her full attention. "When Moni came out to me, I fussed and fumed . . . like an old hen with a chick missing." Katherine smiled. Jean made eye contact again. "But Ken . . . maybe it's a male thing, like so many times when a man's reaction comes from a completely different place than a woman's. I think he sees her sexual preference as a personal rejection. He hasn't been able to separate personal identity from sexuality."

"He is male, therefore he is."

"Exactly. And not liking men sexually equates to not liking men period."

"It's not about disliking men. It has nothing to do with men. It's all about loving a woman."

"But men are used to *everything* being relative to them."

"Mmm," Katherine nodded. "Feminists like you must be particularly frustrating to them. You still want an intimate relationship."

"Yes, but not on their terms."

* * * * *

Shayna placed four drinks in the middle of the table and slid them into place. "Why didn't one of you warn me she could dance like that?"

"Like what?" Jean asked.

"Didn't you see her? I felt like a prop out there."

"I guess we were too busy talking," Katherine replied. "Where is she?"

"Someone grabbed her before we could get off the dance floor."

Totally unprepared for what she faced, Moni turned at the grasp of her arm. The eyes that met her pierced a painful track straight to her heart and paralyzed her in midbreath. They left her with no voice, no breath, barely a heartbeat.

"Will you dance with me?" Paige asked.

Moni released the stopped breath, took an almost normal one, and found her voice. "Just like that." *Unbelievable.* The eyes that had haunted her dreams for years never moved. She shook her head. "I'm with friends." *As if I am the one owing explanation for anything.* She ripped her eyes from Paige's, leaving the sting of a Band-Aid torn from tender skin, and turned to leave.

"Please," she said, with the audacity to step closer. "One dance."

Her expression was one of disbelief mixed with annoyance. "Why, Paige?"

"Because there's a bar full of lesbians here and not one of them can dance. Because . . ."

The look in the piercing blue eyes held an honesty

that found the one unprotected place in her heart. *Which will be more painful, staying or walking away?* It really didn't matter. Her eyes had made the decision to stay on their own. "It is sinful." She couldn't help smiling at the puzzled look on Paige's face. "Letting good music go undanced."

A gentle smile turned the corners of Paige's mouth. Moni found herself being pulled into the rhythm of Paige's shoulders, into the rhythm of the dance. For a hazy few seconds she tried to think of a reason to stop — old anger, old hurt, old love — old. She was past it. *Isn't this the chance I've hoped for many times? To show Paige the little girl has grown up? To remind her of what she could have had.* Her movements were reserved enough, the distance she maintained respectable. A dance with an old friend, nothing more. What was the harm?

But the music came alive in Paige Flemming in a way she had almost forgotten. The space between their bodies closed like the force field pulling lead to a magnet. The sparks of their movements, now filling the narrow gap, ignited a familiar excitement. Arms brushed over arms, lips against hair. Breathed on by alcohol-tinged breath, the excitement was tempered now by age and experience but was every bit as volatile as it ever was. And it didn't go unnoticed. When Paige's hand found Moni's thigh in their first clear contact, Moni playfully slapped it away. The responding laughter proved that more than merely a couple of friends were watching.

Moni continued to tease with looks and turns and suggestive moves until Paige would have no more of it. She grabbed her around the waist, pulled her firmly against her, hip to hip, forehead to forehead.

Time for teasing was over. With commanding control, Paige ground them together, rode the primal beat of Moni's thigh, then turned her away only to pull her back into submission seconds later. Through it all Moni's body complied with every command — immediate response to perfect control. Paige's hands took their liberties to the very edge of respectability, traveling at will down Moni's sides, over her hips, across her abdomen, down her thighs. And what they did to her body went beyond all respectability. While Moni's mind reached for justification, her body followed its own master. Only one other woman had been able to command such heat, and she was watching.

Shayna tried in vain to read a reaction in Katherine's face, but she stared ahead at the dancers with no expression.

"I can't believe I've known Moni this long, yet known so little about her," Jean admitted. "I keep getting one surprise after another."

"The only thing that would surprise *me* is if she didn't know that woman," Shayna said, turning her attention once again to a silent Katherine. "You don't dance like that with a stranger."

Katherine didn't have to look to realize both women were waiting for her response. She took a sip from her drink before making eye contact. "If I'm not mistaken" — she looked again toward the floor as the music changed tempo — "she's the woman who brought Moni out."

"Ooh," Jean whispered.

"Right on the dance floor from the looks of things," Shayna said, standing to pull a chair back to the table as Moni returned.

"I hope I haven't embarrassed anyone," Moni said, scanning the waiting faces.

"Not this erotic-loving lesbian," Shayna replied. "But then, I'm not your lover."

Moni looked from Katherine's stoic stare to Jean and back to Katherine. "I'm sorry. I found myself in an awkward position." She took Katherine's hand. "Will you come to the restroom with me?"

Moni leaned against the corner of the dark hallway and pulled Katherine in front of her. She spoke without looking up, her hands still on Katherine's waist. "I guess I don't have to tell you who that was."

"Like Matthew said, 'Anyone with a seventy IQ.' "

"I didn't know what to do." Her eyes finally searched out their forgiveness. "Part of me wanted to walk away, part of me couldn't."

"Are you still in love with her?"

The question shocked Moni into consideration. *Love? With its fuzzy vision and unbridled passion? The innocent expectation of her youth?*

"I've cheated in my life, Moni, and I've been cheated on. Both are far more painful than truth in the long run . . . I'm asking for honesty."

Moni shifted her weight, pressed the small of her back against the wall. "I still care about her."

"She still turns you on."

"Katherine . . ." The eyes that normally twinkled

with love now held her accountable. They gave her no choice but to admit, "Yes." Then after stripping her naked, Katherine's eyes left her to stare into the smoke-filled darkness.

Moni's reflex came on a shallow breath. "Are *you* being totally honest with me?" Before Katherine could respond, Moni slipped from their private corner and disappeared into the crowd of women.

The inevitable came almost immediately. With the first strains of a classic love song, came the invitation she wasn't sure she was ready for. Paige stopped her as she crossed the corner of the dance floor.

"Not unless we talk, Paige."

"I don't do that very well."

"It takes practice — like dancing."

She wrapped her arms around a reluctant Moni. "I'll try."

Without her willing it, Moni's body registered its awareness of an old familiar excitement. It acknowledged the comfort of the strength embracing it. It flushed at the sensuousness of the breasts pressed around its own. And, guilt ignored, her body liked what it felt. "You have to know something," she said, as her arm was placed around Paige's neck. "I'm no longer single."

Paige said nothing, only embraced her with both arms. As expected, they moved with the music slowly, perfectly. There were no words except those of the song. It was clear that no information, no thought, was going to pass freely.

"Paige —"

"You still make me crazy."

Moni took her arms from Paige's neck, rested her

hands on the broad shoulders. "Yes. You taught me all about that. What it felt like to want, to need, to love. And what it felt like to be left."

Paige dropped her forehead gently against Moni's.

"There's pain deep inside you, too, I know there is," she said, forcing Paige to look at her. "I didn't know then how to tell you I recognized it. I thought love would heal it in you — and in me. But that love brought pain I didn't understand. And pain can make you angry."

"I tried not to hurt you. You would have hated me no matter what I did."

"I did hate you . . . for a while. But mostly I missed you." This time Paige looked willingly into the eyes of the young woman Moni had become. "I loved you, Paige."

"I never wanted you to love me."

"Why?" Paige released her embrace and turned her head, but Moni held her firmly. "No. Not this time."

Paige's eyes came back quickly, sharply, flashing an expression that hinted at anger. But it stopped short at Moni's words. "I need to know, Paige."

"I'm not like you," she said, unable to leave the pleading in Moni's eyes. "You're good."

"And so are you."

"Yeah. Good at dancing — and fucking."

"Stop it."

"I would have destroyed you."

Moni's soul, laden with its burden for so long now that it had grown accustomed to it, suddenly heaved. Freed of the weight at last, it released the bindings on her heart. "Paige, don't . . ." The first noticeable tears rolled slowly from the inside corners of her eyes. "That's not true."

"I couldn't love you. I couldn't love anybody."

"Then what was it that made you worry about me, that made you drive all over the county to get me to games when I didn't have a car, that gave you the patience to work with me until I wasn't afraid . . . that made you lie beside me for months without touching me?"

"I shouldn't have let you get that close. I let you . . . I guess I thought, 'Why not? I deserve something good, too.' " She pulled her head up straight, turned her eyes away to mask the struggle to keep the glaze on her eyes from forming tears. "I knew better."

Moni was shaking her head, cheeks wet with tears. She touched her hand lovingly to the side of Paige's head. "Don't talk like that." The DJ sympathetically rolled straight into another slow song while they stood almost motionless. "You *did* love me — just the way I was. But you never allowed me to do the same."

Paige buried her face against Moni's head. "I couldn't be part of your life. You never would've made it in mine."

"Katherine, give me the word and I'll tell Moni we're taking you home," Shayna offered.

Katherine shook her head. "Awkward situations create an awful ripple effect. I'm sorry you two have to see this. I'm not much good for conversation right now."

"What do you know about this woman?" asked Jean.

"Evidently not enough."

"Despite her sexual appeal, and obvious physical

abilities, she's still just bar action, Katherine," Shayna said.

"If I could believe that, I wouldn't worry. But I know Moni well enough to know there's something much deeper involved."

"Six different cities in four states. Too much alcohol. Too many women with no names." The gate now stood wide open. The exposed path was leading directly to the real Paige Flemming. Moni listened intently. "I woke up one time in the backseat of a car. A gay man I knew was sleeping in the front seat. There was a marriage license on the floor with our names on it. He said I told him I wanted his name." Paige shook her head. "I don't remember how I got there. I don't remember any of it." Moni stared in bewilderment into eyes that now avoided hers. "Booze doesn't do it anymore."

"Doesn't do what?"

"I came back looking for Lou Ann. I wasn't looking for you."

"I'm a big girl now, Paige. Tell me."

"I don't want to run anymore. I'm tired . . . Lou Ann was always there for me before."

"And I'm here now." Moni caressed Paige's head affectionately, and pressed her cheek to Paige's. "You don't have to ask, Paige. Just tell me what you're running from."

She drew a deep breath and forced her eyes back to Moni's. "My real name is Ann Panning." The revelation so surprised her that Moni could do nothing but stare as Paige continued her liberation. "If they ever find me . . ." She saw the shock as it registered in Moni's eyes, and knew she couldn't stop now. "I was fifteen . . . They were going to try me for murder as an adult. So I ran."

"Who?" Moni asked in a whisper.

"My mother's boyfriend . . . I've never said this to anyone."

"It's okay," Moni said, stroking Paige's hair. "It's okay."

"No, it isn't. When women go to prison for murder, Moni, they never come out."

"But it must have been an accident. I can't believe you'd —"

Paige shook her head, while her eyes spanned a distance far beyond the room. "He was sitting at the kitchen table, bellowing that his dinner was cold . . . She stabbed him. Right in the back. She just kept stabbing him, even after he fell to the floor. I had to pry the knife from her hands."

"Your mother?"

Paige's eyes returned from their journey and she nodded.

It was the nod that made the last word of the puzzle fit. "You've been protecting her all this time."

"I told them I did it. We never thought they'd charge a kid . . . She was never much of a mother, between the crack and the men. But she didn't deserve what he did to her."

"No. And you don't deserve what this has done to you."

* * * * *

205

Moni wound between the tables with determination in each step. She reached the table and spoke directly to Katherine. "All right. You stripped me raw," she said with an abrupt shove of the chair. "And I just did the same to Paige." Shayna took Jean's arm and led her discreetly from the table. Moni continued adamantly. "Now it's your turn."

Immutable brown eyes accompanied the stern reply. "Then you'd better tell me what it is you think you don't know."

"What's going on between you and Shayna?"

Katherine sighed and took Moni's stubborn hand. "I knew I should have told you . . . Sit down, Moni."

Fear tightened like a boa around her chest. She pulled her hand from Katherine's. "Just tell me."

"It's not me she's in a tailspin over."

Moni sat down quickly as the realization hit home. She stared into Katherine's eyes. "Jean? Oh my god. It's been Jean . . . all this time. Why didn't I see it?"

"Shayna asked me not to say anything. I was counting on you to figure it out. Maybe if you hadn't been so full of doubt."

"Doubt?"

"Doubting me . . . doubting yourself."

"I'm sorry, Katherine," she said, resting her forehead heavily in the palms of her hands. "I'm so sorry. I've been such an ass."

Katherine tried to take her hand, but Moni would not lift her head. "I should have realized how it would look to you. Look at me, Moni." Moni lifted her head and let Katherine take her hand. "I should have at least told you that Shayna had spoken to me in confidence."

"I was still an ass. Doubting you, teasing Paige. At

my own expense, as well as yours . . . I'm embarrassed at what I'm about to ask of you." Katherine's silence did nothing to help justify her request. "I'm going to need to see Paige alone for a while, and the only reason I can give you is that she trusts no one else."

"Will you sleep with her?"

"No."

"Do you know how hard it was for me to watch you tonight? Knowing that the relationship I was seeing was at one time more than a dance? Wondering whether it would be again?"

Moni stared down at the drink, still untouched in front of her, and placed her mind at the table with Shayna and Jean. She saw what Katherine must have seen, looking out at her lover on the dance floor in the arms of her ex-lover. With their bodies touching intimately, familiarly. She heard the questions, sensed the hurt and the embarrassment Katherine must have felt. "I know it's asking a lot. I know I'm asking for more trust than *I* had in you. If I could take back the pain I caused you, I would. Katherine, I'm finally at a place where I can forgive, and now I need forgiving."

"And you are forgiven. Because you're loved," she said, gently lifting Moni's gaze to her own. "As long as we're honest with each other, we'll be all right." She traced her fingers tenderly over Moni's cheek. "Your devotion is one reason I fell in love with you. I've known that about you from the beginning. I trust you to do what you have to, Moni."

"You're the one I'm in love with, Katherine," she said, retrieving an envelope from her jacket and placing it in Katherine's hands. "The only one."

"What's this?"

"Something I was saving for later, for among the

207

boxes." She watched the gentle smile that formed on Katherine's lips as she opened the letter. "It's a job offer. Close enough so that you'll take the position at Braxton. I want to spend the rest of my life with you."

"Are you sure I'm what you need? That I'm exciting enough for you?"

"I'm sure." She smiled with endearment at the thought that this woman would have even the slightest worry of pleasing her. "What you do to me physically and emotionally . . ." She left her seat and settled onto Katherine's lap. "You know what you give me that's more important than anything else? What I've prayed for all my life?" Katherine's eyes rested in the loving gaze. "You give me mornings-after filled with the love you promised the night before."

Katherine's lips were warm and tender. She kissed her openly for the first time, confirming her love for her without fear. The feeling made Moni almost giddy. She hugged Katherine and let go of a half-stifled laugh.

"What?"

"Jean!" She smiled, tilting her head back. "I can't believe I've been missing all the fun."

A few of the publications of
THE NAIAD PRESS, INC.
P.O. Box 10543   Tallahassee, Florida 32302
Phone (850) 539-5965
Toll-Free Order Number: 1-800-533-1973
Web Site: WWW.NAIADPRESS.COM
Mail orders welcome. Please include 15% postage.
Write or call for our free catalog which also features an
incredible selection of lesbian videos.

SIXTH SENSE by Kate Calloway. 224 pp. 6th Cassidy James
mystery.   ISBN 1-56280-228-3 $11.95

DAWN OF THE DANCE by Marianne K. Martin. 224 pp. A dance
with an old friend, nothing more . . . yeah!   ISBN 1-56280-229-1   11.95

WEDDING BELL BLUES by Julia Watts. 240 pp. Love, family,
and a recipe for success.   ISBN 1-56280-230-5   11.95

THOSE WHO WAIT by Peggy J. Herring. 160 pp. Two
sisters . . . in love with the same woman.   ISBN 1-56280-223-2   11.95

WHISPERS IN THE WIND by Frankie J. Jones. 192 pp. "If you
don't want this," she whispered, "all you have to say is 'stop.' "
                                                ISBN 1-56280-226-7   11.95

WHEN SOME BODY DISAPPEARS by Therese Szymanski.
192 pp. 3rd Brett Higgins mystery.   ISBN 1-56280-227-5   11.95

THE WAY LIFE SHOULD BE by Diana Braund. 240 pp. Which
one will teach her the true meaning of love?   ISBN 1-56280-221-6   11.95

UNTIL THE END by Kaye Davis. 256pp. 3rd Maris Middleton
mystery.   ISBN 1-56280-222-4   11.95

FIFTH WHEEL by Kate Calloway. 224 pp. 5th Cassidy James
mystery.   ISBN 1-56280-218-6   11.95

JUST YESTERDAY by Linda Hill. 176 pp. Reliving all the
passion of yesterday.   ISBN 1-56280-219-4   11.95

THE TOUCH OF YOUR HAND edited by Barbara Grier and
Christine Cassidy. 304 pp. Erotic love stories by Naiad Press
authors.   ISBN 1-56280-220-8   14.95

WINDROW GARDEN by Janet McClellan. 192 pp. They discover
a passion they never dreamed possible.   ISBN 1-56280-216-X   11.95

PAST DUE by Claire McNab. 224 pp. 10th Carol Ashton
mystery.   ISBN 1-56280-217-8   11.95

CHRISTABEL by Laura Adams. 224 pp. Two captive hearts and
the passion that will set them free.   ISBN 1-56280-214-3   11.95

PRIVATE PASSIONS by Laura DeHart Young. 192 pp. An
unforgettable new portrait of lesbian love . . .   ISBN 1-56280-215-1   11.95

BAD MOON RISING by Barbara Johnson. 208 pp. 2nd Colleen
Fitzgerald mystery.   ISBN 1-56280-211-9   11.95

RIVER QUAY by Janet McClellan. 208 pp. 3rd Tru North
mystery.   ISBN 1-56280-212-7   11.95

ENDLESS LOVE by Lisa Shapiro. 272 pp. To believe, once
again, that love can be forever.   ISBN 1-56280-213-5   11.95

FALLEN FROM GRACE by Pat Welch. 256 pp. 6th Helen Black
mystery.   ISBN 1-56280-209-7   11.95

THE NAKED EYE by Catherine Ennis. 208 pp. Her lover in the
camera's eye . . .   ISBN 1-56280-210-0   11.95

OVER THE LINE by Tracey Richardson. 176 pp. 2nd Stevie
Houston mystery.   ISBN 1-56280-202-X   11.95

JULIA'S SONG by Ann O'Leary. 208 pp. Strangely
disturbing . . . strangely exciting.   ISBN 1-56280-197-X   11.95

LOVE IN THE BALANCE by Marianne K. Martin. 256 pp.
Weighing the costs of love . . .   ISBN 1-56280-199-6   11.95

PIECE OF MY HEART by Julia Watts. 208 pp. All the
stuff that dreams are made of —   ISBN 1-56280-206-2   11.95

MAKING UP FOR LOST TIME by Karin Kallmaker. 240 pp.
Nobody does it better . . .   ISBN 1-56280-196-1   11.95

GOLD FEVER by Lyn Denison. 224 pp. By author of *Dream
Lover.*   ISBN 1-56280-201-1   11.95

WHEN THE DEAD SPEAK by Therese Szymanski. 224 pp. 2nd
Brett Higgins mystery.   ISBN 1-56280-198-8   11.95

FOURTH DOWN by Kate Calloway. 240 pp. 4th Cassidy James
mystery.   ISBN 1-56280-205-4   11.95

A MOMENT'S INDISCRETION by Peggy J. Herring. 176 pp.
There's a fine line between love and lust . . .   ISBN 1-56280-194-5   11.95

CITY LIGHTS/COUNTRY CANDLES by Penny Hayes. 208 pp.
About the women she has known . . .   ISBN 1-56280-195-3   11.95

POSSESSIONS by Kaye Davis. 240 pp. 2nd Maris Middleton
mystery.   ISBN 1-56280-192-9   11.95

A QUESTION OF LOVE by Saxon Bennett. 208 pp. Every
woman is granted one great love.   ISBN 1-56280-205-4   11.95

RHYTHM TIDE by Frankie J. Jones. 160 pp.   . . . to desire
passionately and be passionately desired.   ISBN 1-56280-189-9   11.95

PENN VALLEY PHOENIX by Janet McClellan. 208 pp. 2nd
Tru North Mystery.   ISBN 1-56280-200-3   11.95

BY RESERVATION ONLY by Jackie Calhoun. 240 pp. A
chance for true happiness.   ISBN 1-56280-191-0   11.95

OLD BLACK MAGIC by Jaye Maiman. 272 pp. 9th Robin
Miller mystery.   ISBN 1-56280-175-9   11.95

LEGACY OF LOVE by Marianne K. Martin. 240 pp. Women
will do anything for her . . .   ISBN 1-56280-184-8   11.95

LETTING GO by Ann O'Leary. 160 pp. Laura, at 39, in love
with 23-year-old Kate.   ISBN 1-56280-183-X   11.95

LADY BE GOOD edited by Barbara Grier and Christine Cassidy.
288 pp. Erotic stories by Naiad Press authors.   ISBN 1-56280-180-5   14.95

CHAIN LETTER by Claire McNab. 288 pp. 9th Carol Ashton
mystery.   ISBN 1-56280-181-3   11.95

NIGHT VISION by Laura Adams. 256 pp. Erotic fantasy romance
by "famous" author.   ISBN 1-56280-182-1   11.95

SEA TO SHINING SEA by Lisa Shapiro. 256 pp. Unable to resist
the raging passion . . .   ISBN 1-56280-177-5   11.95

THIRD DEGREE by Kate Calloway. 224 pp. 3rd Cassidy James
mystery.   ISBN 1-56280-185-6   11.95

WHEN THE DANCING STOPS by Therese Szymanski. 272 pp.
1st Brett Higgins mystery.   ISBN 1-56280-186-4   11.95

PHASES OF THE MOON by Julia Watts. 192 pp. . . . . hungry
for everything life has to offer.   ISBN 1-56280-176-7   11.95

BABY IT'S COLD by Jaye Maiman. 256 pp. 5th Robin Miller
mystery.   ISBN 1-56280-156-2   10.95

CLASS REUNION by Linda Hill. 176 pp. The girl from her
past . . .   ISBN 1-56280-178-3   11.95

DREAM LOVER by Lyn Denison. 224 pp. A soft, sensuous,
romantic fantasy.   ISBN 1-56280-173-1   11.95

FORTY LOVE by Diana Simmonds. 288 pp. Joyous, heart-
warming romance.   ISBN 1-56280-171-6   11.95

IN THE MOOD by Robbi Sommers. 160 pp. The queen of
erotic tension!   ISBN 1-56280-172-4   11.95

SWIMMING CAT COVE by Lauren Douglas. 192 pp. 2nd
Allison O'Neil Mystery.   ISBN 1-56280-168-6   11.95

THE LOVING LESBIAN by Claire McNab and Sharon Gedan.
240 pp. Explore the experiences that make lesbian love unique.
                                              ISBN 1-56280-169-4   14.95

COURTED by Celia Cohen. 160 pp. Sparkling romantic
encounter.   ISBN 1-56280-166-X   11.95

SEASONS OF THE HEART by Jackie Calhoun. 240 pp. Romance
through the years.   ISBN 1-56280-167-8   11.95

K. C. BOMBER by Janet McClellan. 208 pp. 1st Tru North
mystery.   ISBN 1-56280-157-0   11.95

LAST RITES by Tracey Richardson. 192 pp. 1st Stevie Houston
mystery.   ISBN 1-56280-164-3   11.95

EMBRACE IN MOTION by Karin Kallmaker. 256 pp. A whirlwind
love affair.   ISBN 1-56280-165-1   11.95

HOT CHECK by Peggy J. Herring. 192 pp. Will workaholic Alice
fall for guitarist Ricky?   ISBN 1-56280-163-5   11.95

OLD TIES by Saxon Bennett. 176 pp. Can Cleo surrender to a
passionate new love?   ISBN 1-56280-159-7   11.95

LOVE ON THE LINE by Laura DeHart Young. 176 pp. Will Stef
win Kay's heart?   ISBN 1-56280-162-7   11.95

DEVIL'S LEG CROSSING by Kaye Davis. 192 pp. 1st Maris
Middleton mystery.   ISBN 1-56280-158-9   11.95

COSTA BRAVA by Marta Balletbo Coll. 144 pp. Read the book,
see the movie!   ISBN 1-56280-153-8   11.95

MEETING MAGDALENE & OTHER STORIES by
Marilyn Freeman. 144 pp. Read the book, see the movie!
                                          ISBN 1-56280-170-8   11.95

SECOND FIDDLE by Kate 208 pp. 2nd P.I. Cassidy James
mystery.   ISBN 1-56280-169-6   11.95

LAUREL by Isabel Miller. 128 pp. By the author of the beloved
Patience and Sarah.   ISBN 1-56280-146-5   10.95

LOVE OR MONEY by Jackie Calhoun. 240 pp. The romance of
real life.   ISBN 1-56280-147-3   10.95

SMOKE AND MIRRORS by Pat Welch. 224 pp. 5th Helen Black
Mystery.   ISBN 1-56280-143-0   10.95

DANCING IN THE DARK edited by Barbara Grier & Christine
Cassidy. 272 pp. Erotic love stories by Naiad Press authors.
                                          ISBN 1-56280-144-9   14.95

TIME AND TIME AGAIN by Catherine Ennis. 176 pp. Passionate
love affair.   ISBN 1-56280-145-7   10.95

PAXTON COURT by Diane Salvatore. 256 pp. Erotic and wickedly
funny contemporary tale about the business of learning to live
together.   ISBN 1-56280-114-7   10.95

INNER CIRCLE by Claire McNab. 208 pp. 8th Carol Ashton
Mystery.   ISBN 1-56280-135-X   11.95

LESBIAN SEX: AN ORAL HISTORY by Susan Johnson.
240 pp. Need we say more?   ISBN 1-56280-142-2   14.95

WILD THINGS by Karin Kallmaker. 240 pp. By the undisputed
mistress of lesbian romance.   ISBN 1-56280-139-2   11.95

THE GIRL NEXT DOOR by Mindy Kaplan. 208 pp. Just what you d expect. ISBN 1-56280-140-6   11.95

NOW AND THEN by Penny Hayes. 240 pp. Romance on the westward journey. ISBN 1-56280-121-X   11.95

HEART ON FIRE by Diana Simmonds. 176 pp. The romantic and erotic rival of *Curious Wine*. ISBN 1-56280-152-X   11.95

DEATH AT LAVENDER BAY by Lauren Wright Douglas. 208 pp. 1st Allison O'Neil Mystery. ISBN 1-56280-085-X   11.95

YES I SAID YES I WILL by Judith McDaniel. 272 pp. Hot romance by famous author. ISBN 1-56280-138-4   11.95

FORBIDDEN FIRES by Margaret C. Anderson. Edited by Mathilda Hills. 176 pp. Famous author's "unpublished" Lesbian romance. ISBN 1-56280-123-6   21.95

SIDE TRACKS by Teresa Stores. 160 pp. Gender-bending Lesbians on the road. ISBN 1-56280-122-8   10.95

WILDWOOD FLOWERS by Julia Watts. 208 pp. Hilarious and heart-warming tale of true love. ISBN 1-56280-127-9   10.95

NEVER SAY NEVER by Linda Hill. 224 pp. Rule #1: Never get involved with . . . ISBN 1-56280-126-0   11.95

THE WISH LIST by Saxon Bennett. 192 pp. Romance through the years. ISBN 1-56280-125-2   10.95

OUT OF THE NIGHT by Kris Bruyer. 192 pp. Spine-tingling thriller. ISBN 1-56280-120-1   10.95

LOVE'S HARVEST by Peggy J. Herring. 176 pp. by the author of *Once More With Feeling*. ISBN 1-56280-117-1   10.95

THE COLOR OF WINTER by Lisa Shapiro. 208 pp. Romantic love beyond your wildest dreams. ISBN 1-56280-116-3   10.95

FAMILY SECRETS by Laura DeHart Young. 208 pp. Enthralling romance and suspense. ISBN 1-56280-119-8   10.95

INLAND PASSAGE by Jane Rule. 288 pp. Tales exploring conventional & unconventional relationships. ISBN 0-930044-56-8   10.95

DOUBLE BLUFF by Claire McNab. 208 pp. 7th Carol Ashton Mystery. ISBN 1-56280-096-5   10.95

BAR GIRLS by Lauran Hoffman. 176 pp. See the movie, read the book! ISBN 1-56280-115-5   10.95

These are just a few of the many Naiad Press titles — we are the oldest and largest lesbian/feminist publishing company in the world. We also offer an enormous selection of lesbian video products. Please request a complete catalog. We offer personal service; we encourage and welcome direct mail orders from individuals who have limited access to bookstores carrying our publications.

LOOKING FOR NAIAD?

Buy our books at
www.naiadpress.com

or call our toll-free number
1-800-533-1973

or by fax (24 hours a day)
1-850-539-9731